HORSE TAILS

Traditional tales, fables and legends from around the world about or featuring our equine friends ...

Compiled, Adapted & Edited by Clive Gilson

Tales from the World's Firesides

Horse Tails, edited by Clive Gilson, Solitude, Bath, UK

www.clivegilson.com

First published in 2025

Printed by IngramSpark

ISBN: 978-1-915081-50-6

CONTENTS

Preface

The First Appearance Of The Horse In Aino-land

How The Horses Of The Sun Ran Away

The Squirrel And The Horse

Ivan And The Chestnut Horse

Pegasus, The Horse With Wings

The Flaming Horse

The Tale of Arion, the Horse of Storms and Song

The Spirit Horse

Binoculars, Bag And Horse

Council Of The Horses

The Girl With The Horse's Head

The Tale of the Hippocampus: Steed of the Sea God

The Tale of Sleipnir, the Horse of Odin

The Fox And The Horse

Uchchaihshravas: The Celestial Horse of the Gods

The Horse Blank

The Horses Of Diomedes

Sigurd's Escape On The Wonderful Horse Gullfaxi

The Speaking Horse

The Wings of Chollima

The Wonderful Horse

The Magician's Horse

The Peasant And The Horse

Epona of the Silver Mane

The Goat And The Horse

The Black Horse

The Tale of the Kiger Mustang

Tradition Of The Finding Of Horses

Brother Fox Catches Mr Horse

The Wax Horse

The Steed of the Night Journey

The Demon Horse Race

The Horse And The Olive

The Tale of the Wind Horse

The Fire-Bird, The Horse Of Power, And The Princess Vasilissa

The Dun Horse

The Salt-Breath of the Nuckelavee

The Story Of The Horse, The Lion, And The Wolf

The Sun-Horse

The Backwards Riders of Storr Rock

Theo And His Horses; Jane, Betsy, And Blanche

Bayard, The Magical Horse

Alastair na Bèisde and the Loch of the Woman

The War Horse Of Alexander

The Hooves of Heaven

Pegasus, The Winged Horse

Story Of The Race Between The Elephant And The Horses

Virgil And The Bronze Horse

The Song of Hayagrīva

The Story Of The Half-Man-Riding-On-The-Worse-Half-Of-A-Lame-Horse

The Horse And His Rider

Pomo And The Goblin Horse

Concerning A Horse

The Two Horses

Y Ceffyl Dŵr - The Water Horse

The First White Flame

The Unicorn

About The Editor

Preface

I've been collecting and telling stories for a couple of decades now, and in more recent years, I've had the joy of seeing some of my own fiction published. I tend to focus on short stories that dip into magical realities and science fiction fantasies, worlds where the strange feels natural and the impossible makes perfect sense.

Folk and fairy tales have always been at the heart of my work. Over the years, I've gathered thousands of them from all around the world. It's been a long-standing dream of mine to create a kind of library, a collection that brings together these incredible stories of people and places from every corner of the globe.

One of my biggest motivations for this project is the desire to preserve tales that might otherwise be forgotten. A lot of the stories I work with come from early collectors, people writing in the late 1700s, through the 1800s, and into the early 20th century. Because of the time in which they were collected, these stories often carry worldviews that can feel uncomfortable or outdated today, especially around themes like race and gender. I do my best to adapt them with care, making them more accessible for a modern reader while staying as true as I can to the spirit of the original.

I also want to be clear that I make every effort not to speak over or appropriate from the cultures these tales come from. Many early collectors made assumptions about the communities they documented, often through a colonial lens. My aim is to preserve and share the stories as respectfully as possible. To that end, I've included proper attributions for every tale, identifying the original collector or author, the source it was taken from, and, wherever possible, the cultural or indigenous origins of the story.

This particular volume, *Horse Tails*, is a collection of folk and fairy tales from around the world where horses take centre stage. Aside from the obvious admiration many of us feel for these majestic creatures, I found that there are so many good reasons to bring these horse-centred stories together.

Horses hold a special place in the stories of countless cultures. They've been companions in peace, partners in war, symbols of beauty, freedom, strength, and sometimes magic. Including them in folklore makes the stories feel familiar and emotionally rich, no matter where they come from.

As you might expect, horses in these tales are often noble, brave, and loyal, sometimes mysterious, even divine. But there are also darker, more complex stories, as no folk tradition is complete without a shadow or two. Together, they reflect the deep and varied relationships humans have had with horses through time.

Many of these stories carry moral lessons, teaching us about courage, trust, wisdom, and endurance through the adventures and trials their horse-heroes face. Like all good fairy tales, they invite us into enchanted worlds where animals speak, stars fall, and the right kind of kindness can break a curse.

And perhaps most beautifully, these tales are part of the great oral tradition that lives within every culture. By sharing them, we keep alive not just the stories, but also the values, beliefs, and dreams of the people who first told them.

There's something profoundly human in the act of storytelling. Since the earliest days, when we gathered around fires in caves and imagined what it meant to be alive, we've shared tales of magic, cleverness, danger, and love. As I've explored stories from the Celts, from Indonesia, from Africa and the Far East, truly from everywhere, I've been struck again and again by how deeply connected we all are. Our stories may wear different clothes, but underneath, they share the same bones.

These horse tales, like all folk stories, carry joy and sorrow, light and shadow. Some are wild and wonderful. Others are quiet and tender. But all of them, in some way, are part of us. I've loved collecting and retelling them, and I hope you find something magical in them too.

With warmth and wonder,

Clive

Bath 2025

The First Appearance Of The Horse In Aino-land

A Japanese Tale

This tale is adapted from Basil Hall Chamberlain's book Aino Folk-Tales, published by The Folk-lore Society, London, in 1888. This tale was translated literally as told by Penri on the 12th of July 1886.

Basil Hall Chamberlain (1850 – 1935) was a British scholar best known for his work on Japanese language, literature, and folklore during the Meiji era. He wasn't a "folklorist" in the modern, fieldwork-heavy sense. He was more of a philologist and translator who also collected and published folk tales.

A very beautiful woman had a husband. He was a very skilful fellow. Once he went to the mountains, and disappeared. But at night he returned, bearing a deer on his back.

After feasting on the deer, they went to bed. But in the middle of the night, the woman wept and screamed, saying, "This man is not my husband. Though with shame, I will declare the fact as it is. His penis is so big, so big, so big, that it will not get into my vagina; and if it did get in, I should die."

Alarmed by her cries, the neighbours ran out, and came into her house; and one strong fellow took a stick, and beat the husband, saying, "You must be some sort of devil," whereupon the husband turned into a horse, and ran away neighing.

Afterwards he was beaten to death. The truth was that the husband had been killed and supplanted by the horse. That was the first the Ainos saw of horses.

In ancient days every sort of creature could thus assume human shape. So it is said.

How The Horses Of The Sun Ran Away

A Greek Tale

This tale is adapted from Mary Catherine Judd's book Classic Myths, published by Allyn and Bacon, in 1901.

Mary Catherine Judd (1852 – 1930) was an American educator and folklorist known for adapting myths, legends, and nature stories for children. A former school principal in Minneapolis, she believed storytelling could teach moral lessons and foster a love of nature.

Phaeton had always been told he was the son of Helios, god of the Sun. He'd heard it from his mother, Clymene, so many times that it burned in him like a dare. One day, he finally said,

"Mother, I'm going to see him, face to face."

She nodded. "Then go east to the place where the Sun rises. Ask him for a gift. He'll know you're his son."

That night, Phaeton tightened the straps on his sandals, pulled on a heavier silk robe, and set out toward the land of sunrise, which people now call India. He walked for days and nights without tiring, his robe never too hot, his sandals never worn.

Eventually, he climbed the highest peak on earth and saw the palace of the Sun, its towers blazing with gold and precious stones. He climbed endless stairs, passing walls painted and carved with oceans and cities, forests and rivers, mermaids riding fish, and stars etched into the ceiling. Finally, at the top, the silver doors flew open, flooding him with a light so intense it forced him to stop.

Inside, Helios sat on a diamond throne, cloaked in crimson, the air shimmering around him. Beside him stood the Days and Months, hand in hand, while the Seasons waited in their turn, Spring crowned in flowers, Summer draped in roses, Autumn with grape-stained feet, and Winter in frost and ice.

Helios's gaze pierced him. "Why are you here?"

"My father," Phaeton said, voice trembling, "grant me one request, so that all will know you are truly mine."

Helios, moved, set aside his crown of rays and embraced him. "Ask what you will, and it's yours."

The words were barely out before Phaeton answered, "Let me drive your chariot for one day."

Helios's smile faded. "You don't know what you're asking. No god but me, can control those horses. They'll kill you. Choose something else."

"My mother says my father always keeps his promises."

Helios sighed. "So be it."

The chariot gleamed like living sunlight with gold axles, silver spokes, and jewels flashing in every surface. Dawn opened the purple doors of the sky. The Hours led out the horses, restless and wild. Helios bathed Phaeton's face in protective oil, placed the crown of rays on his head, and gave him final advice, "Spare the whip. Hold the reins tight. Keep to the middle path. Too high and you'll burn the heavens, too low and you'll set the earth on fire."

But Phaeton, grinning with pride, leapt into the seat and shouted to the horses.

They exploded forward through the morning clouds. On earth, people thought the Sun had risen early and began working double-time. But soon the horses sensed the weakness in their driver and veered off course. Constellations flinched from the heat. Africa scorched black under the blaze, rivers dried, and mountains burned. Even the Nile fled underground.

From the Moon's chariot, Artemis loosed arrows to turn the maddened horses away from smashing her silver car. Earth herself cried out to Zeus, "End this before we all burn!"

Zeus hurled a lightning bolt. Phaeton fell from the sky, spinning like a dying star until he crashed into an Italian river. His sisters wept on the banks until they rooted into poplar trees, leaves trembling forever at the touch of heaven's wind.

The horses, finally soothed, returned to Helios's palace by nightfall. And the Sun rose again the next morning, steady as ever, but without his son.

The Squirrel And The Horse

A Spanish Tale

This is my own version of a tale written originally as verse by Tomás de Iriarte in his book Literary Fables of Yriarte, published by Ticknor And Fields, London, in 1855.

Tomás de Iriarte (1750–1791) was a Spanish neoclassical poet, playwright, and fabulist best known for his witty and didactic fables written in verse. Born in the Canary Islands and later active in Madrid, Iriarte was deeply influenced by Enlightenment ideals and used his literary work to promote reason, education, and moral instruction.

Long ago, in the sun-drenched heart of Andalusia, when olive groves blanketed the hills and shepherds still played reed pipes by their flocks, there lived a noble sorrel steed named Lucero. He belonged to a respected caballero and was famed throughout the region not only for his beauty but for his devotion and skill. His coat shone like polished chestnut, his gait was smooth as river water, and he moved with the quiet power of a divine creature both wild and trained.

One golden afternoon, as Lucero was let loose to exercise in the wide open plain outside the villa, he galloped in wide arcs across the grass. His hooves beat a rhythm against the earth, strong and graceful, as he circled and turned, his every motion full of purpose. Nearby, from the shadow of an old cork tree, a small grey squirrel perched on a stone wall, watching with his bright black eyes.

The squirrel, named Pico, was well-known in the nearby woods for his chatter. Quick of foot and quicker of tongue, he was a creature of tireless movement and tireless opinion.

Pico twitched his tail as Lucero passed by in a smooth canter. Then, springing down from the wall with a flourish, he darted onto the field and called out, "Señor Caballo! A fine show, indeed! Truly, a delight to watch."

Lucero slowed his gallop slightly, ears flicking back in polite acknowledgment.

Pico scampered ahead, running circles in the grass, then leaping to a tree, spiralling up its trunk, and diving back down in a blur.

"You see that?" he said proudly. "I too move with speed and elegance. In fact, I daresay I'm as graceful as you, perhaps more so! My leaps, my twists, my dashes from earth to branch and back again, ¡caramba!, all done with ease. I am never still, always light, always quick. Why, I don't need reins or saddles. I perform for no one and yet move like poetry itself!"

Lucero came to a full stop, his hooves kicking up a soft puff of dust. He turned his head and regarded the squirrel with calm, steady eyes.

"You move well," Lucero said in a voice as even as his stride. "And I see you take pride in your games. But let me ask you, little Pico, for whom do you move? What purpose guides your swiftness?"

Pico blinked. "Purpose? Why, I move because I can! I leap for joy! I dash for fun! Who needs a purpose for beauty?"

Lucero nodded slowly. "Indeed. There is joy in movement for its own sake. But I do not run merely to show how fast I am. When my master calls, I am ready. When the hills are steep or the path uncertain, I carry him with sure footing. When danger nears, I do not dash in circles, I stand firm. I serve rather than just soar. That, little friend, is the difference."

Pico shifted his weight, suddenly less certain. "But still, your elegance is not so different from mine."

Lucero offered a faint, patient smile. "The dance is similar. But the reason we dance is not."

At that, Lucero lifted his head, gave a soft whinny, and trotted back toward the stable, where his master waited with saddle and reins in hand. The squirrel watched him go, his tail flicking thoughtfully.

And from that day on, though Pico still leapt and darted with the same wild energy, he sometimes paused to wonder not just how he moved, but why he moved.

Ivan And The Chestnut Horse

A Russian Tale

This tale is adapted from Edmund Dulac's book Edmund Dulac's Fairy-Book, published by George H. Doran Co., New York, in 1916.

Edmund Dulac (1882–1953) was a French-born, British illustrator celebrated for his opulent, dreamlike artwork during the Golden Age of Illustration. Known for his jewel-toned palettes, intricate patterns, and influences from Persian miniatures, Japanese prints, and Art Nouveau, he brought a distinctive elegance and exoticism to classics such as The Arabian Nights, The Rubáiyát of Omar Khayyám, and The Sleeping Beauty.

In a far land where they pay people to keep its name a profound secret, there lived an old man who brought up his three sons just exactly in the way they should go. He taught them the three R's, and also showed them what books to read and how to read them. He was particularly careful about their education, for he had learned that to know things was to be able to do things.

At last, when he came to die, he gathered his three sons round his deathbed and cautioned them.

"Do not forget," he said, "do not forget to come and read the prayers over my grave."

"We will not forget, father," they replied.

The two elder brothers were great big, strapping fellows, but the youngest one, Ivan, was a mere stripling. As they all stood around their dying father's bed, he looked a mere reed compared to his proud, stout, elder brothers. But his eyes were full of fire and spirit, and the firm expression of his mouth showed great determination. And, when the father had breathed his last, and his two elder brothers wept without restraint, Ivan stood silent, his pale face set and his eyes full of the bright wonder of tears that would not melt.

On the day that they buried their father, Ivan returned to the grave in the evening to read prayers over it. He had done so, and was making his way homeward, when there was a great clatter of hoofs behind him.

Then, as he reached the village square, the horseman pulled up and dismounted quite near to him. After blowing a loud blast on his silver trumpet, for he was the King's messenger, he cried in a loud voice, "All and every man, woman and child, take notice, in the name of the King. It is the King's will that this proclamation be cried abroad in every town and village where his subjects dwell. The King's daughter, Princess Helena the Fair, has caused to be built for herself a shrine having twelve pillars and twelve rows of beams. And she sits there upon a high throne till the time when the bridegroom of her choice rides by. And this is how she shall know him… With one leap of his steed he reaches the height of the tower, and, in passing, his lips press those of the Princess as she bends from her throne. Wherefore the King has ordered this to be proclaimed throughout the length and breadth of the land, for if any deems himself able so to reach the lips of the Princess and win her, let him try. In the name of the King I have said it!"

The blood of the youth of the nation, wherever this proclamation was issued, took flame and leapt to touch the lips of Princess Helena the Fair. All wondered to whose lot this lucky fate would fall. Some said it would be to the most daring, others contended that it was a matter of the leaping powers of the steed, and yet others that it depended not only on the steed but on the daring skill of the rider also.

When the three brothers had listened to the King's messenger they looked at one another; at least the elder two did, for it was apparent to them that Ivan, the youngest, was quite out of the competition, whereas they, two splendid handsome fellows, were distinctly in it.

"Brothers," said Ivan at last, "our first thought must be to fulfil our father's dying wish. But, if you prefer it, we could take it in turns to read the prayers over our father's grave. Let it be the duty of one of us each day to fulfil the duty, morning and evening."

The elder brothers agreed readily to this, but, when Ivan asked whose turn it should be on the morrow, they both began to make excuses.

"As for me," said the eldest, "I must go and order the work of the farm my father left me, and that will take seven days."

"And for me," said the younger, "I must see to the estate which is my part of the inheritance, and that also will take seven days."

"Then," replied Ivan, "if I perform the duty for seven days, you will each do your share afterwards?"

His brothers agreed still more readily than before. Then they went their ways, Ivan full of thoughts of his father, and the other two to train their jumping horses, the one on his farm and the other on his estate. And both laughed to themselves, for neither knew the purpose of the other.

How they curled their hair and cleaned their teeth, and practised 'prunes and prisms' with their mouths close to the looking-glass, so that when, at one bound of their magnificent steeds, they reached the level of the Princess's lips, to aim the kiss that was to win the prize, they would make a brave show, and a conquering one. As for their little brother, they each thought he could go on praying over their father's grave as long as he liked, it would be the best thing he could do, and it would not interfere with their secret plans, so carefully concealed from each other and from him.

So, for seven days, in their separate districts, they raced about on their horses by day and dreamed of the greatest leaping feats by night. And at the end of the seven days the youngest brother summoned them to keep their agreement, and asked which of them would read the prayers, morning and evening, for the second seven days.

"I have done my part," he said. "Now it is for you to arrange between you which one shall continue the sacred duty."

The two elder brothers looked at each other and then at Ivan.

"As for me," said one, "I care little who does it, so long as I am free to get on with my business, which is more important."

"And as for me," said the other, "I am in no mind to watch each blade of grass growing on the grave. I cannot really afford the time, I am so busy. You, Ivan, you are different. You are not a man of affairs. How could you spend your time better than reading prayers over our father's grave?"

"So be it," replied Ivan. "You get back to your work and I will attend to the sacred duty for another seven days."

The two elder brothers went their separate ways, and for seven more days devoted their entire attention to training their horses for the flying leap at the Princess's lips. How they tore like mad about the fields! How they jumped the hedges and ditches! How they curled their hair and dyed their moustaches and practised their lips, not only to 'prunes and prisms,' but to 'peaches of passion' and 'pomegranates,' and 'peripatetic perambulation' and everything they could think of. In fact, they paid so much attention to the lips which were to meet those of the Princess at the top of the flying leap, that they began to neglect their own and their horses' meals. In other words, they were beginning to show signs of over-training.

At the end of the second seven days Ivan again summoned them to a family council, and asked them if either of them could now take up the sacred duty. But no. thinking heavily on horses and lips, and high jumps and kisses, they spoke lightly of fields to be tilled, seed to be sown, and all such things that must be done at once. Their view was, and they got quite friendly over it, that Ivan should be more than delighted to bear this pleasurable burden of reading prayers over his father's grave. Indeed, nothing but the stern call of immediate duty would prevail upon them to relinquish a task so pleasant.

"So be it," said Ivan. "I will perform the sacred duty for another seven days." But as he spoke, he noted his brothers' curled hair and dyed moustaches, and gleaned from this, and from the look of sudden suspicion and jealousy exchanged between them, that they were both in love with the same fair one. But he kept this to himself, and left them to their own concerns.

Again, at the end of seven days, when Ivan had read the prayers devoutly, he summoned his brothers. But they did not come. Both sent messages saying that they were frightfully busy, and would he be so good as to go on with the sacred duty until they could be spared to do their share later on. Ivan accepted their messages, and went on reading the prayers over the father's grave.

Meanwhile each of his brothers prepared for the great flying leap, and each said to himself, "What about Ivan? He would like to see this great exploit. It might make a man of him. He is altogether lacking in ambition, and to see a great deed done might stir him to try to be a great hero himself. But yet, I fear it would never do. He is so weedy, so insignificant. I feel I should lose by having a brother like that anywhere about. No; he is far better reading prayers over our father's grave."

So each in his own way resolved to go in alone, apart from the other and apart from Ivan.

The morning of the great day came. The eldest brother had chosen from his horses a magnificent black one with arched neck and flowing mane and tail. The second brother had selected a bay equally splendid. And now, at sunrise, they were, each unknown to the other, combing their well-curled hair, re-dyeing their moustaches, and booting and trapping themselves for the wonderful display of prowess the day was to bring forth. And they did not forget to make sure that their lips were as fit as they were anxious for the 'high kiss.'

At the appointed time they rode into the lists and drew their lots, and neither was altogether surprised at seeing his brother among the host of competitors for the hand of Helena the Fair. Their surprise came later, when Ivan arrived on the scene.

It so happened in this way… Towards evening, when his two brothers had each had their last try to leap up to the Princess's lips and failed, like everyone else, Ivan himself was reading the prayers over his father's grave. Suddenly a great emotion came over him, and he stopped in his reading. He was filled with a longing to look just for once upon the face of Helena the Fair, for whose favour he knew that the most splendid in the land were competing with their wonderful steeds. So strong was this longing that he broke down and, bending over his father's grave, wept bitterly.

And then a strange thing happened. His father heard him in his coffin, and shook himself free from the damp earth, and came out and stood before him.

"Do not weep, Ivan, my son," he said. And Ivan looked up and was terrified at the sight of him.

"No, my son, do not fear me," his father went on. "You have fulfilled my dying wish, and I will help you in your trouble. You wish to look upon the face of Helena the Fair, and so it shall be."

With this he drew himself up, and his aspect was commanding. Then he called in a loud voice, and, as the echoes of his tones began to die away, Ivan heard them change into the far-distant beat of a horse's hoofs. After listening for a while his father called again, and this time the echo was a horse's neigh and galloping hoofs. It seemed to come from beyond the hillside, and Ivan looked up and wondered. A third time his father called, and nearer and nearer came the galloping sound, until at last, with a thundering snort and a ringing neigh, a beautiful chestnut horse appeared, circled round them three times, and then came to a halt before them, its two forefeet close together and its eyes, ears, and nostrils shooting flames of fire.

Then came a voice, and Ivan knew it was the voice of the chestnut horse with the proudly arched neck and flowing mane. "What is your will? Command me and I obey!"

The father took Ivan by the hand and led him to the horse's head. "Enter here at the right ear," he said, "and pass through, and make your way out at the left ear. By so doing you will be able to command the horse, and he will do whatever you may wish that a horse should do."

So Ivan, nothing doubting, passed in at the right ear of the chestnut horse and came out at the left, and immediately there was a wonderful change in him. He was no longer a dreamy youth. He was at once a man of affairs, and the light of a high ambition shone in his eyes.

"Mount! Go, win the Princess Helena the Fair!" said his father, and then he immediately vanished.

With one spring Ivan was astride the chestnut horse, and, in another moment, they were speeding like lightning towards the shrine of Helena the Fair. The sun was setting, and the two elder brothers, disconsolate, were about to withdraw from the field, when, startled by the cries of the people, they saw a steed come galloping on, well ridden, and at a terrific pace. They turned to look and they marked how Helena the Fair, disappointed of all others, leaned out to watch the oncoming horseman. And the whole concourse turned and stood to await the possible event.

On came the chestnut horse, his nostrils snorting fire, his hoofs shaking the earth. He neared the shrine, and, to a masterful rein, rose at a flying leap. The daring rider looked up and the Princess leaned down, but he could not reach her lips, ready as they were.

The whole field now stood at gaze as the chestnut horse with its rider circled round and came up again. And this time, with a splendid leap, the brave steed bore its rider aloft so that the fragrant breath of the Princess seemed to meet his nostrils, and yet his lips did not meet hers.

Again they circled round while all stood still and tense. Again the chestnut steed rose to the leap, and, this time, Ivan's lips met those of the Princess in a long, sweet kiss, for the chestnut horse seemed to linger in the air at the top of its leap while that kiss endured.

Then, while the Princess looked after, horse and rider reached the ground and disappeared like lightning.

Instantly the host of onlookers swarmed in. "Who is he? Where is he?" was the cry on every hand. "He kissed her on the lips, and she kissed him. Look at her! Is it not true?"

It was true, for Princess Helena the Fair, with a lovelight in her eyes, was leaning down and searching, with all her soul, even for the very dust spurned from the heels of her lover's horse. But she could see nothing, and sank back within her shrine, treasuring the kiss upon her lips while the people, dissatisfied, but wondering greatly, melted away. Among them went the splendid brothers, seeking how they could sell their well-trained horses to advantage, for they had both been frantically near to the Princess's lips.

Where had Ivan flown on the chestnut horse? Loosing the reins, he cared for nothing but the kiss, and he let his steed go, and presently it came to a standstill before his father's grave. There he dismounted and turned the horse adrift. As if its errand was completed, it galloped off, and a rainbow came down to meet it, and, closing in, seemed to snatch it up in its folds. Ivan was alone before his father's grave.

Once more he bowed himself in prayer. Once more his father appeared before him.

"You have done well, my son," he said. "You have fulfilled my dying wish, but my living wish is yet to be fulfilled. Tomorrow Helena the Fair will summon the people and demand her bridegroom. Be there, but say nothing."

With this Ivan found himself alone.

On the following day there was a great gathering at the palace, and, in the midst of it, sat Princess Helena the Fair demanding her bridegroom, the one who had leapt to her lips and won her from all others. Her heart and soul and body were his. The half of her kingdom to come was his. She, herself, was his, but where was he?

Search was made among the highest in the land, but, fearing a demand for the repetition of the leap and the kiss, none came forward. Ivan sat at the back, a humble spectator.

"She is thinking of that leap and that kiss," he said to himself. "When she sees me as I am, then let her judge."

But love, though blind, has eyes. The Princess rose from her seat and swept a glance over the people. She saw the two handsome elder brothers and passed them by as so much dirt. Then, by the light of love, she descried, sitting in a corner, where the lights were low, the hero of the chestnut horse, the one who had leapt high and reached her lips in the first sweet kiss of love.

She knew him at once, and, as all looked on in wonder, she made her way to that dim corner, took him by the hand without a word, and led him up, past the throne of honour, to an antechamber, where, with the joyous cries of the people ringing in their ears, their lips met a second time, at the summit of a leap of joy.

At that moment the King entered, knowing all. "What is this?" he asked.

Then he smiled, for he understood his daughter, and knew that she had not only chosen her lover, but had won her choice.

"My son," he added, without waiting for an answer, "you and yours will reign after me. Look to it! Now let us go to supper."

Pegasus, The Horse With Wings

A Greek Tale

This tale is adapted from Mary Catherine Judd's book Classic Myths, published by Allyn and Bacon, in 1901.

Mary Catherine Judd's most famous work, Classic Myths (1896), retold Greek, Norse, and other world myths in accessible language for young readers, and she also published collections of nature tales. Judd's work blended education with gentle moral instruction, making her a notable figure in late 19th–early 20th century children's literature.

On Mount Helicon, the nine Muses tended a creature unlike any other, a winged white horse whose feathers shone in the sunlight. Daughters of Zeus, the Muses inspired humankind with music, poetry, history, dance, and knowledge of the stars. Their gift was memory, helping mortals recall the beauty and wisdom they shared.

One summer morning, the horse appeared at the Muses' fountain. Thalia, Muse of Comedy, spotted him first as she descended from the sky. Terpsichore, Muse of Dance, tried to grab his mane, but his wings flashed wide, blinding her for an instant, and he was gone before her fingers touched him.

Urania, Muse of Astronomy, wondered if he came from the stars. Clio, Muse of History, was certain no such creature had ever walked, or flown, on earth before. They named him Pegasus, and he returned to the fountain each morning.

"What is his purpose?" they asked each other. "All things have their work."

They found out soon enough.

Far away in Lycia, a young soldier named Bellerophon was winning too much admiration for his own good. Handsome, bold, and fearless, he stirred envy in those who should have been his friends. His king sent him to deliver a sealed letter to King Iobates of Lycia, not telling him that the letter secretly asked for Bellerophon's death.

For ten days, Iobates treated his guest to feasts and dancing before opening the letter. When he finally read it, he was troubled. He didn't want to kill the young man outright. Then his advisors reminded him of the Chimera, a fire-breathing monster with the head of a lion, the body of a goat, and the tail of a serpent, that was terrorizing the western hills.

Perfect, thought Iobates. If Bellerophon died fighting the beast, his hands would be clean.

He summoned the soldier. "There's a monster ravaging my lands. Will you face it?"

"I will," said Bellerophon without hesitation. "My heart is pure, my strength is as the strength of ten. I fear nothing."

That night, Bellerophon slept in the temple of Athena, goddess of wisdom. In a dream, she came to him with a golden bridle and told him to seek Pegasus at the fountain of Priene.

When he awoke, the bridle was in his hands.

He found Pegasus drinking at the fountain. At the sight of the golden bridle, the horse didn't flee. Bellerophon slipped it over his head and swung onto his back. Pegasus struck the earth once with his hooves, then leapt into the sky, wings slicing the clouds.

The Muses looked up as the rider and horse soared past. "He has found his purpose," said Clio.

From the air, Bellerophon spotted the Chimera. He swooped down, struck, and killed it. For all its legend, the beast was not as invincible as it seemed. Pegasus carried him back to Iobates in a single bound and then vanished to Helicon.

But the king wasn't done testing him. Task after dangerous task was set before Bellerophon, and Pegasus always came when called. Together they succeeded every time.

Eventually, Iobates relented, gave Bellerophon his daughter's hand, and welcomed him into his family. Pegasus remained the beloved companion of the Muses, sometimes carrying them high into the sky, though no mortal but Bellerophon ever dared to ride him.

But the soldier's ambition grew restless. One morning, with no great quest left to conquer, he called Pegasus and decided to ride him to Mount Olympus, home of the gods.

Zeus saw him rising toward the sacred heights and sent a single gadfly to sting Pegasus. The horse flinched, believing the pain came from his rider. Furious, he reared, throwing Bellerophon from his back.

The soldier plummeted to earth, crashing into rocky ground far from any city. He survived, but was blinded and crippled. Separated from friends and honour, he wandered alone until his story faded into obscurity.

Pegasus returned to Mount Helicon and never again came at Bellerophon's call. Yet some say he's still seen at the Muses' fountain, and once in a hundred years, a gifted soul catches the flash of his golden bridle.

The Flaming Horse

A Czechoslovak Tale

This tale is adapted from Parker Fillmore's book Czechoslovak Fairy Tales, published by Harcourt, Brace And Co., New York, in 1919.

Parker Fillmore (1879–1944) was an American writer, translator, and folklorist best known for collecting and adapting folk tales from Eastern Europe, particularly Czech, Slovak, and Finnish traditions, for English-speaking audiences.

There was once a land that was dreary and dark as the grave, for the sun of heaven never shone upon it. The king of the country had a wonderful horse that had, growing right on his forehead, a flaming sun. In order that his subjects might have the light that is necessary for life, the king had this horse led back and forth from one end of his dark kingdom to the other. Wherever he went his flaming head shone out and it seemed like beautiful day.

Suddenly this wonderful horse disappeared. Heavy darkness that nothing could dispel settled down on the country. Fear spread among the people and soon they were suffering terrible poverty, for they were unable to cultivate the fields or do anything else that would earn them a livelihood. Confusion increased until the king saw that the whole country was likely to perish.

In order then, if possible, to save his people, he gathered his army together and set out in search of the missing horse. Through heavy darkness they groped their way slowly and with difficulty to the far boundaries of the kingdom. At last they reached the ancient forests that bordered the neighbouring state and they saw gleaming through the trees faint rays of the sunshine with which that kingdom was blessed.

Here they came upon a small, lonely cottage which the king entered in order to find out where he was and to ask directions for moving forward. A man was sitting at the table reading diligently from a large open book. When the king bowed to him, he raised his eyes, returned the greeting, and stood up. His whole appearance showed that he was no ordinary man but a seer.

"I was just reading about you," he said to the king, "that you were gone in search of the flaming horse. Exert yourself no further, for you will never find him. But trust the enterprise to me and I will get him for you."

"If you do that, my man," the king said, "I will pay you royally."

"I seek no reward. Return home at once with your army, for your people need you. Only leave here with me one of your serving men."

The king did exactly as the seer advised and went home at once. The next day the seer and his man set forth. They journeyed far and long until they had crossed six different countries. Then they went on into the seventh country which was ruled over by three brothers who had married three sisters, the daughters of a witch.

They made their way to the front of the royal palace, where the seer said to his man, "Stay here while I go in and find out whether the kings are at home. It is they who stole the flaming horse and the youngest brother rides him."

Then the seer transformed himself into a green bird and flew up to the window of the eldest queen and flitted about and pecked until she opened the window and let him into her chamber. When she let him in, he alighted on her white hand and the queen was as happy as a child.

"You pretty thing!" she said, playing with him. "If my husband were home how pleased he would be! But he's off visiting a third of his kingdom and he won't be home until evening."

Suddenly the old witch came into the room and as soon as she saw the bird she shrieked to her daughter, "Wring the neck of that cursed bird, or it will stain you with blood!"

"Why should it stain me with blood, the dear innocent thing?"

"Dear innocent mischief!" shrieked the witch. "Here, give it to me and I'll wring its neck!"

She tried to catch the bird, but the bird changed itself into a man and was already out of the door before they knew what had become of him. After that he changed himself again into a green bird and flew up to the window of the second sister. He pecked at it until she opened it and let him in. Then he flitted about her, settling first on one of her white hands, then on the other. "What a dear bird you are!" cried the queen. "How you would please my husband if he were at home. But he's off visiting two-thirds of his kingdom and he won't be back until tomorrow evening."

At that moment the witch ran into the room and as soon as she saw the bird she shrieked out, "Wring the neck of that wretched bird, or it will stain you with blood!"

"Why should it stain me with blood?" the daughter answered.

"The dear innocent thing! Dear innocent mischief!" shrieked the witch. "Here, give it to me and I'll wring its neck!"

She reached out to catch the bird, but in less time than it takes to clap a hand, the bird had changed itself into a man who ran through the door and was gone before they knew where he was. A moment later he again changed himself into a green bird and flew up to the window of the youngest queen. He flitted about and pecked until she opened the window and let him in. Then he alighted at once on her white hand and this pleased her so much that she laughed like a child and played with him.

"Oh, what a dear bird you are!" she cried. "How you would delight my husband if he were home. But he's off visiting all three parts of his kingdom and he won't be back until the day after tomorrow in the evening."

At that moment the old witch rushed into the room. "Wring the neck of that cursed bird!" she shrieked, "or it will stain you with blood."

"My dear mother," the queen answered, "why should it stain me with blood, beautiful innocent creature that it is?"

"Beautiful innocent mischief!" shrieked the witch. "Here, give it to me and I'll wring its neck!"

But at that moment the bird changed itself into a man, disappeared through the door, and they never saw him again. The seer knew now where the kings were, and when they would come home. So he made his plans accordingly. He ordered his servant to follow him and they set out from the city at a quick pace.

They went on until they came to a bridge which the three kings as they came back would have to cross. The seer and his man hid themselves under the bridge and lay there in wait until evening. As the sun sank behind the mountains, they heard the clatter of hoofs approaching the bridge. It was the eldest king returning home. At the bridge his horse stumbled on a log which the seer had rolled there.

"What scoundrel has thrown a log here?" cried the king angrily.

Instantly the seer leaped out from under the bridge and demanded of the king how he dared to call him a scoundrel. Clamouring for satisfaction he drew his sword and attacked the king. The king, too, drew sword and defended himself, but after a short struggle he fell from his horse dead. The seer bound the dead king to his horse and then with a cut of the whip started the horse homewards.

The seer hid himself again and he and his man lay in wait until the next evening. On that evening near sunset the second king came riding up to the bridge. When he saw the ground sprinkled with blood, he cried out, "Surely there has been a murder here! Who has dared to commit such a crime in my kingdom!"

At these words the seer leaped out from under the bridge, drew his sword, and shouted, "How dare you insult me? Defend yourself as best you can!"

The king drew his sword, but after a short struggle he, too, yielded up his life to the sword of the seer. The seer bound the dead king to his horse and with a cut of the whip started the horse homewards.

Then the seer hid himself again under the bridge and he and his man lay there in wait until the third evening. On the third evening just at sunset the youngest king came galloping home on the flaming steed. He was hurrying fast because he had been delayed. But when he saw red blood at the bridge he stopped short and looked around. "What audacious villain," he cried, "has dared to kill a man in my kingdom!"

Hardly had he spoken when the seer stood before him with drawn sword demanding satisfaction for the insult of his words.

"I don't know how I've insulted you," the king said, "unless you're the murderer."

When the seer refused to parley, the king, too, drew his sword and defended himself. To overcome the first two kings had been mere play for the seer, but it was no play this time. They both fought until their swords were broken and still victory was doubtful.

"We shall accomplish nothing with swords," the seer said. "That is plain. I tell you what. Let us turn ourselves into wheels and start rolling down the hill and the wheel that gets broken let him yield."

"Good!" said the king. "I'll be a cartwheel and you be a lighter wheel."

"No, no," the seer answered quickly. "You be the light wheel and I'll be the cartwheel."

To this the king agreed. So they went up the hill, turned themselves into wheels and started rolling down. The cartwheel went whizzing into the lighter wheel and broke its spokes.

"There!" cried the seer, rising up from the cartwheel. "I am victor!"

"Not so, brother, not so!" said the king, standing before the seer. "You only broke my fingers! Now I tell you what. Let us change ourselves into two flames and let the flame that burns up the other be victor. I'll be a red flame and you be a white one."

"Oh, no," the seer interrupted. "You be the white flame and I'll be the red one."

The king agreed to this. So they went back to the road that led to the bridge, turned themselves into flames, and began burning each other mercilessly. But neither was able to burn up the other.

Suddenly a beggar came down the road, an old man with a long grey beard and a bald head, with a scrip at his side and a heavy staff in his hand.

"Father," the white flame said, "get some water and pour it on the red flame and I'll give you a penny."

But the red flame called out quickly, "Not so, father! Get some water and pour it on the white flame and I'll give you a shilling!"

Now of course the shilling appealed to the beggar more than the penny. So he got some water, poured it on the white flame and that was the end of the king. The red flame turned into a man who seized the flaming horse by the bridle, mounted him and, after he had rewarded the beggar, called his servant and rode off.

Meanwhile at the royal palace there was deep sorrow for the murdered kings. The halls were draped in black and people came from miles around to gaze at the mutilated bodies of the two elder brothers which the horses had carried home. The old witch was beside herself with rage. As soon as she had devised a plan whereby she could avenge the murder of her sons-in-law, she took her three daughters under her arm, mounted an iron rake, and sailed off through the air.

The seer and his man had already covered a good part of their journey and were hurrying on over rough mountains and across desert plains, when the servant was taken with a terrible hunger. There wasn't anything in sight that he could eat, not even a wild berry. Then suddenly they came upon an apple tree that was bending beneath a load of ripe fruit. The apples were red and pleasant to the sight and sent out a fragrance that was most inviting. The servant was delighted.

"Glory to God!" he cried. "Now I can feast to my heart's content on these apples!" He was already running to the tree when the seer called him back. "Wait! Don't touch them! I will pick them for you myself!"

But instead of picking an apple, the seer drew his sword and struck a mighty blow into the apple tree. Red blood gushed forth. "Just see, my man! You would have perished if you had eaten one apple. This apple tree is the eldest queen, whom her mother, the witch, placed here for our destruction."

Presently they came to a spring. Its water bubbled up clear as crystal and most tempting to the tired traveler. "Ah," said the servant, "since we can get nothing better, at least we can take a drink of this good water."

"Wait!" cried the seer. "I will draw some for you." But instead of drawing water he plunged his naked sword into the middle of the spring. Instantly it was covered with blood and blood began to spurt from the spring in thick streams. "This is the second queen, whom her mother, the witch, placed here to work our doom."

Presently they came to a rosebush covered with beautiful red roses that scented all the air with their fragrance. "What beautiful roses!" said the servant. "I have never seen any such in all my life. I'll go pluck a few. As I can't eat or drink, I'll comfort myself with roses."

"Don't dare pluck them!" cried the seer. "I'll pluck them for you." With that he cut into the bush with his sword and red blood spurted out as though he had cut a human vein. "This is the youngest queen," said the seer, "whom her mother, the witch, placed here in the hope of revenging herself on us for the death of her sons-in-law."

After that they proceeded without further adventures. When they crossed the boundaries of the dark kingdom, the sun in the horse's forehead sent out its blessed rays in all directions. Everything came to life. The earth rejoiced and covered itself with flowers.

The king felt he could never thank the seer enough and he offered him the half of his kingdom. But the seer replied, "You are the king. Keep on ruling over the whole of your kingdom and let me return to my cottage in peace."

He bade the king farewell and departed.

The Tale of Arion, the Horse of Storms and Song

A Greek Tale

This is my own version of a traditional legend, written and adapted from various sources and historical notes in my collection of folk and fairy tales.

The tale comes down to us through Greek epic and tragic traditions, especially in fragments from Stesichorus (6th century BCE), Herodotus (5th century BCE), and later in Pausanias' Description of Greece (2nd century CE). Like many Greek myths, it blends elements of divine birth, animal symbolism, and heroic warfare, with Arion embodying both the storm's fury and the saving grace of music or voice, hence the epithet "Horse of Storms and Song."

When gods still walked among mortals and kings waged war for the favour of Olympus, there was born into the world a horse unlike any other, a steed whose hooves never stumbled, whose flanks shimmered like moonlight on a silver sea, and whose voice could ring as clear as a man's. His name was

Arion, and his tale is woven deep into the fabric of Greek myth.

Arion's origins were no less strange than the creature himself. It is said he was born not of mare and stallion, but through divine craft. According to the ancient poets, Poseidon, god of the sea, once longed for the beauty and wildness of Demeter, goddess of grain and growing things. To escape him, she fled across the lands in the form of a mare. But Poseidon, cunning and relentless, transformed himself into a stallion and overtook her. From that union, half divine, half animal, sprang Arion, not a beast, but something greater, a horse with the strength of the tides and the speed of the northern wind.

He could run faster than any chariot, leap over valleys, and cross plains as if the earth itself bent to his will. His mane was like rippling flame, and his hooves struck sparks from stone. But more than this, Arion was gifted with speech, and he could understand the words of men and gods alike.

Arion's destiny was as mighty as his birth. The divine horse passed through the hands of many legendary figures. He served Copreus, then Adrastus, king of Argos, but it was when Heracles, the great hero of Greece, took hold of Arion's reins that the steed's legend truly began.

Heracles was deep into his labours, weary from years of trials, wrestling death, slaying monsters, cleaning foul stables, and capturing sacred beasts. In need of a mount to carry him swiftly over wild lands and treacherous terrain, Heracles was gifted Arion by the gods themselves, whether from Poseidon, proud of his son, or from Demeter, eager to see her child redeemed in noble service.

With Arion beneath him, Heracles rode like a thunderstorm, swift and relentless. The two were said to be of one mind, hero and steed, each trusting the other beyond doubt. Arion bore Heracles into battle against the fierce Eleans and the centaurs of Arcadia. Not once did his hooves falter, even in the bloodiest charge.

Later, when Arion passed into the service of Adrastus again, he played a role in the fateful war of the Seven Against Thebes. The city was cursed, and the warriors who fought to breach its gates were doomed, one by one, to fall. All perished, except Adrastus, king of Argos, who escaped only because Arion bore him away at the moment of slaughter.

Thus Arion became known not only as the Horse of Heracles, but also the Savior of Kings.

Unlike mortal horses, Arion never aged. He was immortal, a child of gods, forever wandering the borders between the divine and the human realms. Some say he still runs across the plains of Thessaly, his breath misting in the morning light, his mane streaking through the storm clouds. Others believe that Arion returned to the sea, to his father Poseidon, leaping into the waves where his silver hooves churn the tides.

The Spirit Horse

An Irish Tale

This tale is adapted from Thomas Crofton Croker's book Fairy Legends and Traditions of the South of Ireland, published by Lea and Blanchard, Chicago, in 1844.

Thomas Crofton Croker (1798–1854) was an Irish antiquarian, folklorist, and author best known for collecting and publishing Irish fairy tales, legends, and folk traditions during the early 19th century. Croker also contributed to works on Irish history, archaeology, and topography, making him a key, if sometimes controversial, figure in preserving and popularizing Irish folk heritage in the Romantic period.

The history of Morty Sullivan ought to be a warning to all young men to stay at home, and to live decently and soberly if they can, and not to go roving about the world. Morty, when he had just turned fourteen, ran away from his father and mother, who were a mighty respectable old couple, and many and many a tear they shed on his account. It is said they both died heart-broken for his loss. All they ever learned about him was that he went on board a ship bound for America.

Thirty years after the old couple had been laid peacefully in their graves, a stranger came to Beerhaven inquiring after them. It was their son Morty, and, to speak the truth of him, his heart did seem full of sorrow when he heard that his parents were dead and gone, but what else could he expect to hear? Repentance generally comes when it is too late.

Morty Sullivan, however, as an atonement for his sins, was recommended to perform a pilgrimage to the blessed chapel of Saint Gobnate, which is in a wild place called Ballyvourney.

This he readily undertook, and willing to lose no time, commenced his journey the same afternoon. He had not proceeded many miles before the evening came on. There was no moon, and the starlight was obscured by a thick fog, which ascended from the valleys. His way was through a mountainous country, with many cross-paths and byways, so that it was difficult for a stranger like Morty to travel without a guide. He was anxious to reach his destination, and exerted himself to do so, but the fog grew thicker and thicker, and at last he became doubtful if the track he was on led to the blessed chapel of Saint Gobnate. But seeing a light which he imagined not to be far off, he went towards it, and when he thought he was getting close to it, the light suddenly seemed a great distance away, twinkling dimly through the fog. Though Morty felt some surprise at this, he was not disheartened, for he thought that it was a light sent by the holy Saint Gobnate to guide his feet through the mountains to her chapel.

And thus he travelled for many a mile, continually, as he believed, approaching the light, which would suddenly start off to a great distance. At length he came so close as to perceive that the light came from a fire, seated beside which he plainly saw an old woman. Then, indeed, his faith was a little shaken, and much did he wonder that both the fire and the old woman should travel before him, so many weary miles, and over such uneven roads.

"In the holy names of the pious Gobnate, and of her preceptor Saint Abban," said Morty, "how can that burning fire move on so fast before me, and who can that old woman be sitting beside the moving fire?"

These words had no sooner passed Morty's lips than he found himself, without taking another step, close to this wonderful fire, beside which the old woman was sitting munching her supper. With every wag of the old woman's jaw her eyes would roll fiercely upon Morty, as if she was angry at being disturbed, and he saw with more astonishment than ever that her eyes were neither black, nor blue, nor grey, nor hazel, like the human eye, but of a wild red colour, like the eye of a ferret. He was filled with wonder at the old woman's appearance, and stout-hearted as he was, he could not but look upon her with fear, judging, and judging rightly, that it was for no good purpose her supping in so unfrequented a place, and at so late an hour, for it was near midnight.

She said not one word, but munched and munched away, while Morty looked at her in silence. "What's your name?" at last demanded the old hag, a sulphurous puff coming out of her mouth, her nostrils distending, and her eyes growing redder than ever, when she had finished her question.

Plucking up all his courage, "Morty Sullivan," he replied "at your service," meaning the latter words only in civility.

"Ubbubbo!" said the old woman, "We'll soon see about that," and the red fire of her eyes turned into a pale green colour. Bold and fearless as Morty was, he trembled at hearing this dreadful exclamation. He would have fallen down on his knees and prayed to Saint Gobnate, or any other saint, for he was not particular, but he was so petrified with horror, that he could not move in the slightest way, much less go down on his knees.

"Take hold of my hand, Morty," said the old woman, "I'll give you a horse to ride that will soon carry you to your journey's end."

So saying, she led the way, the fire going before them. It is beyond mortal knowledge to say how, but on it went, shooting out bright tongues of flame, and flickering fiercely.

Presently they came to a natural cavern in the side of the mountain, and the old hag called aloud in a most discordant voice for her horse! In a moment a jet-black steed started from its gloomy stable, the rocky floor ringing with a sepulchral echo with the clanging hoofs.

"Mount, Morty, mount!" she cried, seizing him with supernatural strength, and forcing him upon the back of the horse. Morty finding human power of no avail, muttered, "O that I had spurs!" and tried to grasp the horse's mane, but he caught at a shadow. Nevertheless, the horse bore him up and bounded forward with him, now springing down a fearful precipice, now clearing the rugged bed of a torrent, and rushing like the dark midnight storm through the mountains.

The following morning Morty Sullivan was discovered by some pilgrims (who came that way after taking their rounds at Gougane Barra) lying on the flat of his back, under a steep cliff, down which he had been flung by the Phooka. Morty was severely bruised by the fall, and he is said to have sworn on the spot, by the hand of O'Sullivan (and that is no small oath), never again to take a full quart bottle of whisky with him on a pilgrimage.

Binoculars, Bag And Horse

A Danish Tale

This tale is adapted from Evald Tang Kristensen's book Fra Mindebo: Jyske Folkeaventyr, published by The author's publisher, Aarhus, in 1898.

Evald Tang Kristensen (1843–1929) was a pioneering Danish folklorist and ethnographer best known for his extensive efforts to collect and preserve the oral traditions of rural Denmark during the late 19th and early 20th centuries.

Once, in a small market town, there lived a herdsman who tended all the cattle for the townsfolk. Every morning, people from the city would drive their cows out to him, and he'd take them into the pastures as had been done for generations. When the herdsman grew older, his young son began helping him.

The boy never learned any other trade. He never ran errands or took on other work. People gossiped about him, saying it was a shame he did nothing else, that he would never be more than the herdsman's boy.

One day, tired of the talk and hungry for more from life, the boy made up his mind to leave.

"I don't want to stay here anymore," he told his father. "I want to go out into the world and see what's there."

The old herdsman frowned. "If you go, I can't manage the herd alone. I'd have to give up my work, and then I'd have no income."

But the boy had already decided. "Tomorrow, I leave," he said, and the next morning he bid his father farewell and set out on foot.

He walked for days, searching for work, but found nothing. Then, one afternoon, he came upon a wild and sprawling wilderness, mountains and valleys, thick forests, and tangled undergrowth. There, among the rocks, he met a man tending sheep.

"What are you doing here?" the boy asked.

"You can see for yourself," the man replied. "I'm watching my sheep."

"What's your name?"

"They call me the Mountain Man. And you?"

The boy explained that he was traveling, looking for work.

"I could use a helper," the Mountain Man said.

"Is the work hard?"

"No. You'll eat well, drink well, live comfortably, and have no responsibilities."

The boy, thinking this a fine offer, agreed and followed the Mountain Man. They walked to a dark cave set deep in the mountains.

"This is my home," the Mountain Man said, leading him inside.

Waiting there was an old woman, the Mountain Man's mother. The Mountain Man grinned at her and said, "I've brought someone for you to fatten up. Once he's plump enough, we'll slaughter and eat him."

The old woman nodded. She put the boy in a small room and fed him nothing but sweet milk, wheat bread, and nuts. Every so often, the Mountain Man would come in, prod his arms and belly, and nod approvingly at his growing weight.

One evening, the boy overheard the Mountain Man say to his mother, "Is he fat enough now?"

"Yes," she replied. "He can't get any fatter."

"Good. Slaughter him tomorrow. It might be a bit of a fight, for he looks strong, but I trust you can handle it."

The old woman agreed.

The next morning, she entered the boy's room and said, "Well, today's the day. Time for you to be slaughtered."

The boy smiled faintly. "All right. How do you want to do it?"

"Come outside and lay your head on this block," she said.

"Why don't you show me how?" the boy suggested.

She bent down and rested her head on the block. In one swift motion, the boy grabbed the axe and struck, killing her instantly. He cut a piece from her, fried it in the pan, and placed it in the corner of the stove, just as she had planned to do to him. Then he arranged her body neatly in bed, placing her head back on the pillow, and fled.

That evening, the Mountain Man returned. Seeing the cooked meat, he ate it, remarking on how good it tasted. Later, he went to speak with his mother, but she didn't answer. When he shook her, her head rolled off the pillow and onto the floor.

Realizing what had happened, the Mountain Man flew into a rage. "That cursed boy tricked you and killed you, and I've eaten my own mother!" he howled. "If I ever find him, he'll pay dearly."

He buried his mother and set off to hunt the boy, cursing his name.

Meanwhile, the boy travelled until he reached a city where a king lived. He asked at the royal stables if there was work, and the stable master hired him. The boy worked hard, and the stable master grew fond of him. Eventually, the stable master went to the king and said, "There's a boy in the stables who's too fine a worker to waste there. I think you should meet him."

The king summoned the boy, liked his manner, and moved him into the kitchens. There too, he excelled, and soon the royal chef told the king the boy was still too good for his station.

The king promoted him again, this time to the royal council. Not everyone was pleased. Other servants grew jealous, fearing the boy might one day outrank them. They went to an old minister and asked him to devise an impossible task for the boy so he might fail and be dismissed.

After some thought, the minister said, "Tell the king the boy claims to know where to find a golden spyglass that can see anything in the world, above or below the earth."

The king summoned the boy and demanded the spyglass. The boy denied ever saying such a thing, but the king insisted, "Bring it to me, or lose your life."

The boy wandered the streets in despair until he met an old woman who asked what troubled him. He told her everything.

"I can help," she said. "I'm a witch. The golden spyglass belongs to the Mountain Man, the same one who once meant to kill you. It sits on a shelf above his head. He sleeps between midnight and one. Go then, and be silent."

The boy did as she instructed, stole the spyglass without waking the Mountain Man, and returned it to the king, who was overjoyed.

But the jealous servants went again to the minister, who invented another task: a magic bag which, when struck on one end, would release endless regiments of soldiers, and when struck on the other, would call them back.

The witch again told the boy it was the Mountain Man's, this time his pillow. The boy retrieved it at midnight and presented it to the king. The bag worked exactly as described.

Still not satisfied, the minister proposed a final challenge: to fetch a horse with a golden bell on every strand of its mane and tail, whose ringing could be heard to the ends of the earth.

The witch told the boy the horse was in the Mountain Man's stable and that they must stuff every bell with cotton before moving it, or the sound would wake him. They succeeded, removed the cotton outside the city, and the horse's music filled the streets.

This time, the king promised the boy anything he wanted.

"I want the old minister hanged," the boy said. "He's been behind every trial you've sent me on."

The king refused, but the boy threatened to use the magic bag against him. Realizing he could not win, the king made peace, offering the boy his daughter's hand and the kingdom.

They were wed in great splendour. Later, the boy returned with the princess to visit his parents. Overjoyed, they wept at the sight of their son as a king. The princess insisted they come live with them in the palace, and they did, in comfort and happiness for the rest of their days.

Council Of The Horses

An English Tale

This is my version of a tale told by Kate Douglas Wiggin and Nora Archibald Smith in their book, The Talking Beasts, published by Houghton Mifflin Company, New York & Boston, in 1911.

This tale is based on a poem by John Gay (1685–1732), an English poet and dramatist best known for his satirical and comic works that critiqued the social and political issues of his time.

Kate Douglas Wiggin (1856–1923) and her sister Nora Archibald Smith (1859–1934) were American authors and educators known for their influential work in children's literature and early childhood education.

Long ago, in a wide and grassy plain where horses lived free and proud, a young colt began to stir unrest among the herd. His coat gleamed like sunlight on a river, and his eyes burned with the fire of youth. Though he had never worn harness nor bit, he had heard stories of saddles, bridles, and ploughs, and he was angry.

"Brothers and sisters," the colt neighed loudly one morning, galloping to the centre of the meadow. "Are we not the strongest of beasts? Our hooves pound the earth like thunder, and our legs can carry us faster than the wind. Why, then, do we bow our heads to man? Why do we let them strap us with leather and iron, ride us, whip us, and work us until our flanks foam and our spirits dim?"

The younger horses stamped and tossed their manes. They had long wondered about such things, and the colt's words sparked fire in their hearts.

"Why should we wear the bit?" he went on. "Why pull their carts and carry their burdens? Are we slaves, born only to serve two-legged masters? Let them first tame the lion and ride the tiger, then come to us. Until then, let us rise and cast off our reins! Let us be as wild as the wind and as free as the deer!"

The meadow rang with whinnies of approval. Even the foals stomped their tiny hooves in support. The Council of Horses was formed that very day, under a great oak, to decide the fate of their kind.

But just as the stirrings of rebellion grew louder, an old horse stepped slowly into the circle. His back was slightly bowed, and his mane was streaked with white. He had once been swift and strong like the colt, and he bore the marks of long work, but his eyes were calm, and his voice was deep.

"I, too, was once young," he said, "and my heart once beat hot with pride. I galloped free, and I cursed the saddle. But hear me now."

The herd quieted, for the old horse had seen many winters and his words carried weight.

"Man may guide us with the rein and drive us with the whip, it is true. But think… who brings us hay when the snow falls thick? Who shelters us from storm and wolf, who tends our wounds, and brushes our coats? Who sows the fields we eat from, and shares the grain with us come harvest? We give our strength to man, yes, but in return, we are fed, housed, and loved. I no longer bear burden, yet I am not cast out. These pastures are mine to graze in peace, a gift from those I once served."

The old horse looked around the circle. "Every creature serves in some way," he said. "The bees serve the flowers. The dogs guard the sheep. Even the mighty tree gives shade. To serve with strength and dignity is no shame."

The wind fell still. The young colt lowered his head, unsure. Then, slowly, he stepped forward and touched his nose to the elder's shoulder.

"I was angry," he said. "Teach me how to serve with pride."

And so, the Council disbanded. The meadow returned to peace. And the colt, like his forebears, was bridled, not as a prisoner, but as a companion.

And thus it is told - he who serves with wisdom may one day lead with honour.

The Girl With The Horse's Head

A Chinese Tale

This story has been adapted from a tale told by Richard Wilhelm in The Chinese Fairy Book, which was originally published by Frederick A. Stokes Co., New York, in 1921.

Richard Wilhelm (1873–1930) was a German sinologist, theologian, and folklorist best known for translating classical Chinese texts into German, including folk tales, philosophy, and spiritual writings. He is especially renowned for his seminal translation of the I Ching (Book of Changes), which introduced Chinese thought to Western audiences and influenced figures like Carl Jung. Wilhelm spent over two decades in China, during which he developed a deep appreciation for Chinese culture and oral traditions.

In the dim ages of the past there once was an old man who went on a journey. No one remained at home save his only daughter and a white stallion. The daughter fed the horse day by day, but she was lonely and yearned for her father.

So it happened that one day she said in jest to the horse, "If you will bring back my father to me then I will marry you!"

No sooner had the horse heard her say this, than he broke loose and ran away. He ran until he came to the place where her father was. When her father saw the horse, he was pleasantly surprised, caught him and seated himself on his back. And the horse turned back the way he had come, neighing without a pause.

"What can be the matter with the horse?" thought the father. "Something must have surely gone wrong at home!"

So he dropped the reins and rode back. And he fed the horse liberally because he had been so intelligent; but the horse ate nothing, and when he saw the girl, he struck out at her with his hoofs and tried to bite her. This surprised the father, so he questioned his daughter, and she told him the truth, just as it had occurred.

"You must not say a word about it to anyone," spoke her father, "or else people will talk about us."

And he took down his crossbow, shot the horse, and hung up his skin in the yard to dry. Then he went on his travels again.

One day his daughter went out walking with the daughter of a neighbour. When they entered the yard, she pushed the horse-hide with her foot and said, "What an unreasonable animal you were, wanting to marry a human being! What happened to you served you right!"

But before she had finished her speech, the horse-hide moved, rose up, wrapped itself about the girl and ran off.

Horrified, her companion ran home to her father and told him what had happened. The neighbours looked for the girl everywhere, but she could not be found.

At last, some days afterward, they saw the girl hanging from the branches of a tree, still wrapped in the horse-hide, and gradually she turned into a silkworm and wove a cocoon. The threads that she spun were strong and thick. Her friend then took down the cocoon and let the poor girl slip out of it, while her friend then she spun the silk and sold it at a large profit.

But the girl's relatives longed for her greatly. To their amazement, one day the girl appeared riding in the clouds on her horse, followed by a great company and she said, "In heaven I have been assigned to the task of watching over the growing of silkworms. You must yearn for me no longer!"

And thereupon they built temples to her in her native land, and every year, at the silkworm season, sacrifices are offered to her and her protection is implored. And the Silkworm Goddess is also known as the girl with the Horse's Head.

The Tale of the Hippocampus: Steed of the Sea God

A Greek Tale

This is my own version of a traditional legend, written and adapted from various sources and historical notes in my collection of folk and fairy tales.

The hippocampus (Greek hippos = horse, kampos = sea monster) was a mythological sea creature with the forepart of a horse and the tail of a fish or serpent. The hippocampus is most strongly associated with Poseidon, god of the sea, who was often depicted riding a chariot drawn by hippocampi. These images appear in Greek art and Roman mosaics as early as the 4th century BCE.

In medieval and Renaissance bestiaries, the hippocampus was reinterpreted as a kind of "real" sea-creature, while in folklore of seafaring nations it took on more fairy-tale qualities, being seen as a magical mount or omen.

Long ago, when the sea was as vast and unknowable as the night sky, there was born in the deepest reaches of Oceanus a creature unlike any other. From the foam of the sea and the breath of the storm came the Hippocampus, a steed with the head and forelegs of a mighty horse and the coiling tail of a great fish, silver-scaled and green-maned, flashing like sunlight on waves.

The first to behold the Hippocampus were the sea-nymphs, the Nereids, who sang to the creature and wove kelp garlands for its mane. They marvelled at its swiftness, for it could leap from wave to wave and dive to the cold abyss with ease. But the creature would not be tamed, and fled from their soft hands into the churning depths.

But the Lord of the Sea, Poseidon Earth-Shaker, saw the Hippocampus rise from the surf like a gleaming god of motion and grace. Wielding his golden trident, Poseidon spoke in the tongue of ocean storms and calmed the wild creature's heart. To him, the Hippocampus bowed, recognizing the commander of the deep.

And so it was that Poseidon, seeking to surpass the chariot of his brother Zeus, drawn by fiery, immortal horses through the sky, called forth not one, but a team of Hippocampi, and yoked them to his chariot of shell and coral. Where they rode, the sea rolled back in a mighty wake, dolphins leapt in tribute, and whales sang hymns in his honour. Their hooves left no prints but stirred the tides, and when they leapt, they became as birds of water and cloud.

To the mortals who stood on rocky coasts and watched the horizon, the passage of Poseidon's chariot was marked by storm-tossed waves and foam like galloping steeds. Sailors swore they glimpsed the great sea-horses pulling their master through the waves, their manes streaming like seaweed, their eyes glowing like pearl and opal.

It was said the Hippocampi also bore the souls of drowned mariners to the gates of the undersea palace in Atlantis, where Poseidon held his court. To see a Hippocampus in a dream was considered an omen of a sea voyage, lucky to some, but a warning to those who had angered the gods.

Legends also tell of a time when Poseidon, in wrath, unleashed his Hippocampi upon a coastal city that had mocked the sea. The creatures rose like a tidal wave, their tails smashing ships and their hooves pounding the earth to salt. The city was drowned and forgotten, but the tale remained.

In later times, the image of the Hippocampus adorned coins, temple carvings, and the prows of ships, a sign of divine protection.

Even now, when the sea is calm and the moon is full, old fishermen claim to see them gliding beneath the surface, drawing invisible chariots along the sea-floor, ever watchful, ever proud, as if awaiting their master's return. For the Hippocampus is no beast of burden. It is a living echo of the divine, half-horse, half-wave, and wholly free.

The Tale of Sleipnir, the Horse of Odin

A Norwegian Tale

This story has been adapted from a tale told by Aemund Sigfusson, who presented the Elder Eddas of Snorre Sturleson in The Elder Eddas of Saemund Sigfusson; and the Younger Eddas of Snorre Sturleson, which was originally published by the Norroena Society, London, in 1906.

Snorre Sturluson (1179–1241) was an Icelandic historian, Skald poet, and politician, best known for preserving much of Norse mythology and early Scandinavian history. As the author of the Prose Edda, a foundational text for understanding Norse myth, and Heimskringla, a sweeping saga of the Norwegian kings, Snorre played a crucial role in shaping the literary and cultural heritage of medieval Scandinavia.

In ancient days, when the gods were new in their halls and the stones of Asgard were yet unweathered by time, there came a mighty smith from Jötunheimr to the gates of the gods. He was tall and cloaked, and his eyes glinted like hoarfrost beneath his hood. He spoke no name, but his craft was great.

He offered to raise a fortress wall around Asgard, stronger than any stonework before or since. He promised that no jötunn nor beast of chaos would breach its gates. Yet he asked a heavy price in return, namely the hand of the goddess Freyja, along with the sun and the moon.

Then spoke Loki, son of Laufey, the trickster and shape-shifter, who never held his tongue when silence was wise. "Let the smith build," said he, "but let it be known that the work must be done in a single winter, and no man may aid him."

The gods agreed, for they trusted not the stranger, and they thought that no man could complete such a task alone. The smith, however, asked only one concession: that he be allowed the help of his horse, Svaðilfari. And this was granted, though it was Loki who spoke for it.

Now it came to pass that the horse Svaðilfari was not like other beasts. It hauled stone as ten teams of oxen, and by the red light of winter's sunless days the wall rose higher and stronger than the gods had feared. The days waned, and the smith's work neared its end.

The gods gathered in counsel. Freyja wept, for she saw her fate sealed. The sun and moon flickered in fear. Then Thor, the red-bearded, raised his hammer, Mjöllnir, and spoke of broken bones and shattered heads. But Odin Allfather, whose word was law, turned his eye upon Loki and said, "This was your bargain. You shall unmake it."

Then Loki, slyest of all, fled the hall and took the shape of a mare, fair and grey. Into the cold night he galloped, and in the moonless woods he called to Svaðilfari in a voice sweet and strange.

The stallion turned from the smith's yoke and gave chase. Through forest and stream he followed the strange mare, and the wall remained unfinished when the last day of winter dawned.

In wrath, the smith struck at the gods, revealing himself as a jötunn in disguise. But Thor was swift with Mjöllnir, and before he could take a step toward Freyja, the smith's skull was split and his bones cast to the wolves.

As for Loki, he returned in time, his eyes downcast and his step weary. For he, who had mocked all things sacred and solemn, had borne a child. That child was Sleipnir, a foal grey as mist and fleet as the storm wind, with eight legs that carried him across the sky and the sea alike.

Odin took the colt and raised it as his own. And in time, Sleipnir became the greatest of all steeds: the swiftest, the surest, the bearer of gods and the guide of the dead. No bridle could bind him, and no path was barred to his hoofs.

Thus it was that from guile and mischief came the noblest of all horses. And Sleipnir bore Odin across the Bifröst, to battle, to wisdom, and even to Hel's dark hall.

And so the tale is told.

The Fox And The Horse

A German Tale

This tale is adapted from Jacob and Wilhelm Grimm's book Children's and Household Tales, published by Realschulbuchhandlung, Berlin, in 1812.

Jacob (1785–1863) and Wilhelm Grimm (1786–1859) were German scholars, linguists, and folklorists whose work helped shape the study of folklore and the modern understanding of fairy tales. They gathered and adapted oral stories from across German-speaking regions, preserving a rich body of folk narratives such as "Cinderella," "Hansel and Gretel," and "Rumpelstiltskin." Although often associated with children's literature, the Grimms saw their work as a scholarly effort to safeguard traditional oral culture, language, and heritage, reflecting their broader interest in philology and German nationalism.

A farmer had a horse that had been an excellent and faithful servant to him, but he was now grown too old to work, so the farmer would give him nothing more to eat, and said, 'I want you no longer, so take yourself off out of my stable. I shall not take you back again until you are stronger than a lion.' Then he opened the door and turned him adrift.

The poor horse was very melancholy, and wandered up and down in the wood, seeking some little shelter from the cold wind and rain. Presently a fox met him, asking "What's the matter, my friend? Why do you hang your head down and look so lonely and woe-begone?"

"Ah!" replied the horse, "justice and avarice never dwell in one house. My master has forgotten all that I have done for him for so many years, and because I can no longer work he has turned me adrift, and says unless I become stronger than a lion he will not take me back again. What chance can I have of that? He knows I have none, or he would not talk so."

However, the fox bade him be of good cheer, and said, "I will help you. Lie down there, stretch yourself out quite stiff, and pretend to be dead."

The horse did as he was told, and the fox went straight to the lion who lived in a cave close by, and said to him, "A little way off lies a dead horse. Come with me and you may make an excellent meal of his carcase."

The lion was greatly pleased, and set off immediately, and when they came to the horse, the fox said, "You will not be able to eat him comfortably here. I'll tell you what, I will tie you fast to his tail, and then you can draw him to your den, and eat him at your leisure."

This advice pleased the lion, so he laid himself down quietly for the fox to tie him to the horse. But the fox managed to tie his legs together and bound them all so hard and fast that with all his strength he could not set himself free. When the work was done, the fox clapped the horse on the shoulder, and said, "Jip! Dobbin! Jip!"

Then up he sprang, and moved off, dragging the lion behind him. The beast began to roar and bellow, till all the birds of the wood flew away for fright, but the horse let him sing on, and made his way quietly over the fields to his master's house.

"Here he is, master," said the horse, "I have got the better of him."

When the farmer saw his old servant, his heart relented, and he said. "You shall stay in your stable and be well taken care of."

And so the poor old horse had plenty to eat, and lived well till he died.

Uchchaihshravas: The Celestial Horse of the Gods

A Hindu Tale

This is my own version of a traditional legend, written and adapted from various sources and historical notes in my collection of folk and fairy tales. The tale of Uchchaihshravas, the celestial horse, originates in ancient Indian mythology, specifically in the Hindu Puranas and the Mahābhārata. The horse is also mentioned in The Bhāgavata Purāṇa and Vishnu Purāṇa, which list him among the treasures (ratnas) that arose from the ocean.

The origin of the tale is Vedic–Puranic cosmology, rooted in the myth of the Churning of the Ocean, with Uchchaihshravas standing as the archetype of the divine horse, supreme among all steeds.

In the earliest of ages, before the world took the form we now know, when gods and demons still vied for supremacy in the vastness of the cosmos, the universe stood on the brink of decay. The nectar of immortality, amrita, had been lost in the depths of the Kshira Sagara, the vast Ocean of Milk. Without its divine elixir, even the gods, the Devas, began to weaken, while the Asuras, the demons of shadow and ambition, grew in strength and arrogance.

Desperate to restore balance and renew their might, the Devas approached the preserver of the worlds, the serene and mighty Lord Vishnu, who dwelt in Vaikuntha on the coils of the great serpent Ananta-Shesha.

"There is only one way," said Vishnu, his voice as calm as still water but heavy with fate. "You must churn the Ocean of Milk and extract from its depths the treasures of eternity, the amrita, the elixir of life. But you cannot do it alone."

And so the Devas, with reluctant hearts, brokered a truce with the Asuras. They would work together, gods and demons, to churn the cosmic ocean, and when the amrita emerged, they would share in its spoils.

For their churning rod, they uprooted the mighty Mount Mandara. For the rope, they bound the cosmic serpent Vasuki around it. The gods held one end, the demons the other, and with great effort and fury, they began to churn the ocean as one churns curd to make butter.

As the ocean swirled and foamed, terrible poisons rose first. most deadly among them was Halahala, which could destroy all creation. The gods recoiled in fear, but Lord Shiva, the great ascetic and destroyer, stepped forward and drank the venom to save the world, holding it in his throat. From that moment, his neck bore the bluish hue of sacrifice, and he was called Neelkantha, the Blue-Throated One.

After the poison came marvels and wonders, gems, goddesses, trees of paradise, celestial animals, and riches beyond mortal imagination. Among them was Lakshmi, goddess of wealth and fortune, who emerged from the ocean to become the consort of Vishnu.

But none shone more brightly than Uchchaihshravas.

From the white froth of the ocean's surge rose a horse of impossible beauty, a stallion of such blinding brilliance that the heavens themselves dimmed in comparison. He was Uchchaihshravas, the "neighing one of high fame," the king of all horses. His coat was pure white, his mane flowed like silver clouds, and from his sides sprouted vast wings of light, so that he soared not only across the earth but across the very winds and stars.

The gods and demons gasped at the sight of him. Born of the ocean's divine churn, Uchchaihshravas embodied majesty, speed, and celestial power.

"Mine!" cried Indra, the King of the Devas, and before any could protest, he mounted Uchchaihshravas and claimed him as his vaahana, his divine steed. The horse neighed once, a sound like rolling thunder across the three worlds, and submitted to the King of the Heavens.

But not all were pleased. Bali, king of the Asuras, seethed with envy. "Why," he shouted, "should the horse go to the gods alone? We churned the ocean together! Why should Indra claim all the treasures?"

Discord grew, and the fragile truce teetered on collapse. But Lord Vishnu, ever the protector, took the form of the beguiling Mohini, a celestial enchantress, and diverted the attention of the Asuras. He ensured the amrita fell into the hands of the Devas, restoring their strength and sealing their victory.

Still, Uchchaihshravas remained a source of contention. Though he became the steed of Indra, stories later tell that the demon king Bali may have claimed him at one point, for he, too, was a great and noble ruler before his fall.

Some texts even say that Uchchaihshravas was offered to the Ashvins, the twin horsemen gods of healing and dawn, while others suggest he was shared among divine beings, racing across the heavens, carrying gods to battle, or ferrying sages to the abodes of enlightenment.

Uchchaihshravas was not a mere beast, he was the archetype of all horses, the model from which every noble steed on earth was shaped. When a horse whinnies before battle or gallops without fear into danger, it is said that Uchchaihshravas's spirit rides with it.

The Horse Blank

A Danish Tale

This tale is adapted from Evald Tang Kristensen's book Fra Mindebo: Jyske Folkeaventyr, published by The author's publisher, Aarhus, in 1898. This tale was told originally by Roland Peder Andreassen and Slotved Fattiggaard.

Evald Tang Kristensen (1843–1929) was a pioneering Danish folklorist and ethnographer renowned for his extensive fieldwork in collecting and preserving the oral traditions of rural Denmark. Over the course of his life, he gathered more than 25,000 folk tales, songs, legends, riddles, and sayings directly from farmers, labourers, and village storytellers, often traveling on foot and writing everything down by hand.

About fifty years ago, there lived a king in Spain. He was a widower, but in time he remarried, taking a young wife.

One day, the young queen went into the forest for an afternoon's amusement. She never returned. A witch had taken her.

The king had a servant who had boasted that it would not be impossible for him to recover the queen. The king heard of it and kept the claim in mind.

A few days later, the king's son, the child of his first wife, was also taken by a witch. When the servant heard this, he again made a show of confidence, claiming he could also recover the prince, if rewarded well for his trouble. This rumour reached the king, and he sent for the man at once.

When the servant stood before him, the king asked, "Is it true you have said you can bring back my wife and my son?"

"Yes," the man replied. "I believe I can, but I will need eight days to discover where the witch lives."

The king agreed, and the man went away, but once alone he began to feel the weight of what he had promised. One day, while wandering the forest in frustration, he sat down and wept.

A witch appeared beside him and asked, "Why do you cry, my son?"

He told her the whole story from beginning to end.

"Here is what you must do," the witch said. "Go back to the king and demand twelve thousand silver coins, for the road is long and hard. Demand also twelve teams of horses, each with its own driver. You will need twelve cows or oxen, it matters not which, slaughtered, quartered, and loaded on a wagon along with their hides. You must not touch the meat or skins until you reach your destination.

"The witch you seek lives south of the Sun, north of the Wind, and west of the Tower of Babylon. When you are half a mile from her home, she will send wolves, bears, and other beasts to devour you. You must throw them the meat instead.

"When you reach her, demand the queen and the prince. She will first test whether you know any magic from the black school. She will transform the prince into a horse and place him among twenty-five others. Choose not the finest, but the ugliest, for that will be him.

"She will then turn the queen into a loaf of wheat bread, placed among many others. Take the one in the middle, and draw your knife as if to cut it. She will cry out, and reveal herself. Then you will have them both."

The man returned to the king and said he was ready to set out, but the journey would be long and difficult. He asked for twelve thousand silver coins, twelve teams of horses with drivers, and twelve cows or oxen. The king provided them. The man then slaughtered the cattle, cut the meat into pieces, loaded it and the hides onto a wagon, and began his journey.

He travelled for a long time. At last, they neared the witch's lands, and the beasts came, hundreds of them, wolves and bears, closing in fast. The man ordered his drivers to throw out meat as quickly as they could. Piece after piece they flung until the beasts were satisfied, and the way ahead was clear.

They reached the witch's dwelling, and the man demanded the queen and the prince, threatening to put a ring in the witch's nose for three years if she refused. She said she would hand them over only if he passed her tests.

First, she led him to the stable where twenty-five beautiful horses stood. "Find the king's son," she said.

The man looked them over. "These fine animals would collapse under me in a moment," he said. "I will take this old, thin mule."

"You are correct," said the witch. "That is the prince. But I have another test. Tomorrow I will turn the queen into wheat bread. You must find her."

The next day, she set many loaves before him. The man pointed to the one in the middle, drew his knife, and said he would cut it.

"Don't cut me," cried the loaf. "Here I am!" It was the queen.

"Still, I have one more test," the witch said. "In the forest runs a wild horse. If you can catch it, you may take the queen and the mule home."

The man went to the mule. "If you were truly the king's son, you could advise me, but you are only a mule."

"I am the king's son," the mule replied. "Dig a hole in the forest the size of my body. Place me in it, cover me with the hides you brought, then with twelve barrels of horseshoe nails, and finally with mulch. Remove my bridle and keep it with you. Stand nearby and jingle it. The wild horse, whose name is Blank, will come in a rage and stamp down onto the hides, thinking to crush me. But he will sink into the skins and stand still. Then you may bridle him and ride him to the witch. Keep me as a mule until we are home. I will tell you then how to make me human again."

The man did as he was told. Blank came thundering through the forest, stamping down into the trap. The man bridled him and mounted, while others pulled the mule from the hole, and then they returned to the witch.

"I have no more tests for you," she said. "You are wiser than I am. I have never caught that horse."

The man bought twenty-four more oxen, slaughtered them, and kept the meat. When they neared the beasts again, they threw the meat to them until it was gone. With still some distance left, the man told the other drivers to abandon their carts and join him on his wagon, leaving the spare horses for the wolves. Thus they crossed the border safely.

In the king's forest, they rested. The man laid next to the queen side by side, placing his sword between them. A passing traveller recognised them and ran to the king, who came at once. Seeing the sword between his queen and the man, the king said, "I intended to kill you, but I see you are innocent. You have brought my queen, but where is my son?"

"I will bring him to you in the morning," the man replied.

The next day, the mule said, "Now you must cut off my head, turn it to face backward, and set it on again."

The man obeyed, and at once the most handsome prince appeared where the mule had stood. The man brought him to the king.

"It is my son," the king declared. "For your trouble, you may have anything you desire."

And so they lived in glory from that day, with a wedding feast and great joy.

The Horses Of Diomedes

A Greek Tale

This tale is my own version, based on a heavily adapted story from Mary E. Burt and Zénaïde A. Ragozin's book Herakles, the Hero of Thebes, and Other Heroes of the Myth, published by Charles Scribner's Sons, London & New York, in 1900.

Mary E. Burt and Zénaïde A. Ragozin were 19th-century educators and folklorists who contributed to children's historical and literary education by adapting ancient tales and legends for young readers. Mary E. Burt was known for her emphasis on moral and literary development in children, often using classic texts and folklore as educational tools. Zénaïde A. Ragozin, a Russian-American scholar and historian, specialised in making the myths, epics, and early histories of Eastern and Near Eastern civilisations accessible to Western audiences.

This Is The Eighth Labour Of Heracles

The morning mist clung to the harbour of Tiryns like the breath of sleeping gods, and Heracles stood at the water's edge, watching his companions ready the black-hulled ship.

The salt air carried whispers of the task ahead, whispers that made even hardened sailors ward off the evil eye and mutter prayers to Poseidon. This would be no ordinary voyage.

Eurystheus had summoned Heracles three days prior, his thin lips curved in that familiar smile that spoke of malice wrapped in royal decree. "Your eighth labour, cousin," he had announced from behind his bronze shield, cowering as always in Heracles' presence. "The mares of Diomedes. Bring them to my stables."

The very mention of that name had sent a chill through the throne room. Diomedes was the Storm King, son of Ares, whose realm of Thrace lay beyond the civilised world like a festering wound on the northern border of Greece. Even the boldest warriors spoke his name in hushed tones, for his cruelty was legendary, and his horses were an abomination that defied the natural order.

Now, as Heracles watched his faithful companions, Abderus, young and eager, and Iolaus, steadfast as always, and a dozen others who had sworn to follow him even unto death, he felt the familiar weight of responsibility settle upon his shoulders like Zeus's own aegis. How many would return? How many mothers would weep for sons lost to his cursed labours?

"The ship is ready, my lord," called Abderus, his youthful face bright with anticipation. At nineteen, the boy still saw adventure where older men saw only death. He had been Heracles' cup-bearer in Thebes, volunteering eagerly for this quest when others had found sudden urgent business elsewhere.

Heracles nodded, shouldering his great club and the lion's skin that had become his armour and his burden. "Then let us sail before the wind changes its mind about favouring us."

The voyage north took five days, each one carrying them further from the sun-blessed lands of Greece and deeper into waters that grew progressively darker and more violent. The crew spoke little as they rowed, understanding that each league brought them closer to a land where the very gods seemed turned against humanity.

On the fourth night, as they sheltered in a cove beneath towering cliffs, old Argus the navigator pulled Heracles aside. The weathered sailor's eyes held the accumulated wisdom of forty years at sea, and his expression was grave.

"I've sailed these waters before, son of Zeus," he said quietly, mindful of sleeping ears. "Twice I've seen the Thracian coast, and twice I've fled rather than make landfall. The very stones of that country seem to thirst for blood. But the horses..." He shuddered. "I've heard the screaming on the wind. Not the screaming of men being killed, but of men being eaten alive."

Heracles gazed north, where the aurora painted the sky in sheets of green and gold. "What manner of horses are they, truly?"

"No natural beasts," Argus replied. "They say Diomedes made a pact with his father Ares, and fed the god the flesh of a hundred prisoners to transform ordinary mares into something that craves human meat above grass or grain. Their teeth are like a shark's, rows of them, and their eyes..." He fell silent, unable to continue.

"Their eyes?"

"Like looking into the Pit itself. Red as fresh blood, and they know. Somehow, they know they're committing an evil thing, and they glory in it."

The next morning brought them within sight of Thrace. The coastline rose before them like a mouthful of broken teeth, with jagged black rocks and sheer cliffs that seemed to lean inward, ready to crush any vessel that dared approach. Above the precipices, dark forests stretched to the horizon, broken only by columns of smoke that marked the hill-forts of the native tribes.

But it was the sound that truly announced their arrival in Diomedes' realm. Even from a mile offshore, they could hear it, a sound that was not quite wind, not quite animal cry, but something that raised the hair on every neck and sent ice through every heart. It was hunger given voice, appetite become audible, and it seemed to emanate from the very stones of the coast.

"The stables," whispered Iolaus, his usual courage visibly shaken. "We can hear them from here."

Heracles studied the shoreline through narrowed eyes. A single harbour broke the hostile coast, dominated by a fortress of black stone that squatted like a spider on the heights above. From its walls flew banners bearing the boar's head of Diomedes, and even at this distance, they could see the glint of bronze from the guards on the battlements.

"There," he pointed to a smaller cove, perhaps half a mile west of the main harbour. "We land there, under cover of darkness. Argus, you and two men stay with the ship. Have her ready to sail the moment we return."

"And if you don't return?" the old sailor asked quietly.

Heracles smiled grimly. "Then sail for home and tell them we tried."

As the sun died behind the Thracian mountains, painting the sky the colour of blood, they made their approach. The black water seemed to resist their passage, and more than once the oarsmen swore they saw shapes moving beneath the surface, pale, reaching things that might have been the drowned souls of Diomedes' victims.

They beached the ship on a narrow strand of black sand, hauling it up beyond the tide line and camouflaging it with driftwood and seaweed. Then, armed and as silent as hunting wolves, they began the ascent toward Diomedes' fortress.

The path was treacherous, winding through stands of twisted pines that seemed to whisper warnings in languages older than Greek. Twice they had to flatten themselves against the rock face as Thracian patrols passed, their bronze-scaled armour clanking like chains as they searched the darkness for intruders. It was near midnight when they finally crested the ridge and saw their destination.

The stables of Diomedes stretched across a natural amphitheatre in the rock, a series of stone buildings arranged around a central courtyard. But these were no ordinary stables. Each stall was built like a prison cell, with bronze bars as thick as a man's wrist and doors that looked more suited to holding wild beasts than horses. The sound that had haunted them from the sea was clearer now, a constant, hungry growling punctuated by the scrape of hooves and the rattle of chains.

And there, moving between the stalls like a master reviewing his prized collection, walked Diomedes himself. The Storm King was a giant of a man, nearly as tall as Heracles and broader across the shoulders. His hair was the colour of dried blood, bound back with gold rings, and his beard was braided with the finger bones of his enemies. He wore armour of black bronze that seemed to absorb the moonlight, and at his side hung a sword whose blade was stained dark with old killings.

But it was his eyes that marked him as something more than mortal. They held the same cruel intelligence that Heracles had seen in his divine stepmother Hera, the cold calculation of one who delighted in suffering for its own sake. This was a man who fed strangers to his horses not from necessity, but from love of the act itself.

As they watched from the shadows, Diomedes approached one of the stalls and began speaking to its occupant in the guttural Thracian tongue. The response was not the whinny of a horse, but a sound that was part growl, part scream, and entirely unnatural.

"By the gods," breathed Abderus. "What has he done to them?"

The question was answered as Diomedes stepped back and unlocked the bronze gate. The creature that emerged was still recognisably a horse, but only just. It stood nearly seven feet at the shoulder, its coat the colour of dried blood. Its mane had grown coarse and wild, more like a lion's than a horse's, and when it opened its mouth to nuzzle its master's hand, they could see rows of sharp, pointed teeth like a shark's.

The eyes that were the worst thing, though, as red as rubies, and bright with an intelligence that was not quite animal but certainly not human. They held a malevolent awareness that spoke of understanding exactly what they were, and taking pleasure in the horror they inspired.

Diomedes produced something from a leather bag at his belt, a human hand, freshly severed. The mare took it delicately between her teeth and began to chew, the sound of crunching bones echoing across the courtyard like a death rattle.

"Four of them," whispered Iolaus, counting the stalls. "Four mares of Hell itself."

Heracles nodded grimly. The names were carved into bronze plaques above each door: Podargos, Lampon, Xanthos, and Deinos, also known as Swiftfoot, Shining One, Yellow, and Terrible. Each name seemed to pulse with malevolent life in the moonlight.

"The guards?" asked one of their companions, a grizzled warrior named Lycaon.

They counted perhaps twenty men scattered around the complex, some on the walls, others moving through the courtyard. All were heavily armed and bore the scarred, brutal look of men who lived by violence. But they seemed almost secondary to the real guardians of this place, the mares themselves, whose supernatural senses would detect any intruder long before mortal guards could react.

Heracles studied the layout, his tactical mind working through possibilities. The stables were built into the natural rock, with only one way in or out, that being the main gate. The walls were too high to scale while leading horses, and the guards were too numerous to overcome quietly. It would have to be a direct assault, swift and brutal.

"Abderus," he said quietly. "You'll stay here with half the men. When you see us emerge with the horses, bring the ship around to the main harbour. We'll need to move fast, for every Thracian warrior for miles will be converging on us."

The young man's face fell. "But lord, I want to fight beside you…"

"You are fighting beside me," Heracles said firmly. "Your task is no less vital than mine. Without the ship ready, we all die here."

The assault began an hour before dawn, when the guards were weariest and the darkness deepest. Heracles led the charge, his great club crushing the first sentry's skull before the man could cry out. But stealth was impossible once they crossed the threshold. The mares sensed them immediately, erupting into a cacophony of inhuman screams that raised every warrior in the fortress.

The battle that followed was like something from the darkest myths. Heracles fought his way through the courtyard like a force of nature, his club shattering bronze armour and crushing bones with each swing. Iolaus guarded his left flank, his sword work precise and deadly, while Lycaon and the others formed a protective circle around the stable doors.

But the Thracians fought with the desperate fury of men defending their own territory. They poured from the fortress above, arrows whistling through the night air, spears glinting in the torchlight. And worst of all, Diomedes himself came striding into the melee like some primordial war god, his great sword carving through Heracles' men as if they were wheat before the sickle.

"Free the horses!" Heracles roared, parrying a spear thrust and countering with a blow that sent his attacker flying into the stone wall. "Get them to the harbour!"

But the mares of Diomedes were no ordinary beasts to be led with gentle words and soft hands. The moment their bronze gates swung open, they erupted from their stalls like furies from Tartarus itself. Podargos trampled a Thracian warrior, then bent to tear the flesh from his bones with her terrible teeth. Lampon's eyes blazed like crimson stars as she charged into a knot of defenders, her hooves striking sparks from the stone as she scattered them like leaves.

Xanthos and Deinos followed, their mouths already bloody with the taste of battle. They were not fleeing, they were hunting, and the courtyard became an abattoir as they fell upon friend and foe alike with equal hunger.

"The chains!" Iolaus shouted over the din of battle. "They still wear their chains!"

It was true. Each mare bore bronze shackles around her legs, connected by lengths of chain that Diomedes had used to restrain them in their stalls. But now those same chains became the means of control, if they could seize them.

Heracles ducked beneath Diomedes' sword, feeling the black blade whistle past his ear, and lunged for Podargos' trailing chain. His lion-skin protected him from her snapping teeth as he wrapped the bronze links around his wrist, using his tremendous strength to force the mare's head down.

"To me!" he bellowed to his surviving companions. "Take the chains!"

What followed was perhaps the strangest battle in all the long catalogue of heroic deeds. While Thracian warriors pressed their attack from all sides, the Greeks fought to capture supernatural horses that were themselves as dangerous as any enemy. Lycaon managed to grab Lampon's chain but was nearly dragged to his death when the mare tried to leap onto the stable roof. Another warrior, young Phaistos, seized Xanthos only to scream as the mare's teeth tore through his armour and into his shoulder.

And through it all, Diomedes pressed his attack on Heracles, his sword work revealing the skill of one trained from birth in the arts of war. He was strong, perhaps not quite as strong as the son of Zeus but close enough to make the contest deadly. More dangerous still was his speed, for the Storm King fought with the fluid grace of a dancer, his blade seeming to be everywhere at once.

"You think to steal my beauties, Greek?" Diomedes snarled as their weapons locked together. "They will feast on your bones before the sun rises!"

Heracles said nothing, saving his breath for the fight. But he could see the truth in the Thracian king's eyes. This was not about horses or honour or royal command. This was about the simple joy Diomedes took in causing suffering. He loved his mares not despite their monstrousness, but because of it.

The turning point came when Heracles managed to drive Diomedes back against one of the stable doors. The Storm King, confident in his skill, attempted a complex disarming manoeuvre that left him momentarily exposed. Heracles' club took him in the ribs, lifting him from his feet and hurling him against the stone wall with bone-crushing force.

Diomedes slumped to the ground, his black armour cracked, blood streaming from his mouth. But his red eyes still blazed with defiant hatred as Heracles approached.

"Kill me then, son of Zeus," he gasped. "But know that my father Ares will have his revenge."

Heracles hefted his club, then paused. Around them, the battle was winding down. Most of the Thracian defenders were dead or had fled, and his surviving companions had managed to secure three of the four mares. Only Deinos remained free, circling the courtyard like a wolf seeking an opening to attack.

An idea formed in Heracles mind, terrible in its justice, but perfect in its irony.

"Your mares are hungry," Heracles said quietly. "They should be fed."

Understanding dawned in Diomedes' eyes, followed immediately by fear, the first real emotion other than cruelty that Heracles had seen in him. "No," the Storm King whispered. "Not... not like this."

But Heracles had already seized him, lifting the broken king as easily as a child might lift a doll. Diomedes' strength, formidable as it was, meant nothing against the son of Zeus. His struggles were pitiful, his pleas falling on ears that had heard too many cries from his victims to hold any sympathy.

Heracles carried him to where Deinos waited, the terrible mare's eyes fixed on the approaching meal with unmistakable hunger. Her teeth gleamed like ivory daggers in the torchlight, and a low growling sound emerged from deep in her throat.

"Please," Diomedes begged, all his royal arrogance stripped away by the proximity of the death he had dealt to so many others. "I'll give you gold, slaves, anything you desire…"

Heracles released him directly in front of the mare.

What followed was mercifully brief. Diomedes' screams echoed across the courtyard for perhaps thirty seconds before they cut off abruptly. Deinos fed with the methodical efficiency of a creature that had performed this act many times before, and when she finally looked up from her meal, her muzzle dark with blood, she seemed somehow calmer.

It was Iolaus who noticed it first. "Look at her eyes," he said wonderingly.

The terrible red glow was fading from Deinos's gaze, replaced by something that was still wild but no longer supernatural. As they watched in amazement, the same transformation began to overtake the other mares. Podargos shook her great head as if waking from a dream, while Lampon's muscles began to lose their unnatural bulk.

"The curse," breathed Lycaon. "It's breaking."

Heracles nodded slowly, understanding dawning. "They were not born monsters. Diomedes made them so, feeding them human flesh until it became their only craving. But when fed with their master..." He smiled grimly. "Perhaps the spell breaks with its caster."

Indeed, as the minutes passed, the mares continued to change. Their teeth remained sharp but no longer looked like rows of daggers. Their eyes cleared to a more normal brown, though still wild and dangerous. They were still far from ordinary horses, but no longer the supernatural horrors they had been.

The transformation was not complete. They would always be dangerous, always carry the taint of what they had been forced to become, but they could be controlled now, led by strong hands and brave hearts rather than simply chained like wild beasts.

The retreat to the harbour was a nightmare of its own. Diomedes' death had been seen from the fortress above, and horn calls were already echoing across the Thracian hills. Soon every warrior tribe for miles would be converging on them, seeking revenge for their fallen king.

They moved as quickly as they dared, the mares now docile enough to be led but still requiring constant vigilance. Twice they had to fight their way through hastily assembled forces of Thracian warriors, and each battle cost them men they could not spare.

By the time they reached the harbour, only half their original force remained. Abderus waited with the ship as promised, but his young face was tight with worry as he watched the dawn sky lighten behind the pursuing enemies.

"Quickly!" Heracles ordered. "Get them aboard!"

Loading four supernatural horses onto a Greek warship proved to be a challenge unlike any they had faced in battle. The mares, despite their transformation, remained massive and powerful beasts with tempers to match. Podargos nearly kicked a hole in the ship's hull before they managed to secure her in the makeshift stalls they had prepared. Lampon broke her restraints twice and had to be wrestled down by four men.

But finally, impossibly, they were aboard and ready to depart. The harbour entrance beckoned like salvation itself, and beyond it lay the open sea and the long journey home.

It was then that the Thracian fleet appeared.

A dozen black ships rounded the headland in tight formation, their bronze rams gleaming in the morning sun, their decks crowded with warriors thirsting for revenge. At their head sailed a vessel larger than the rest, flying the golden boar's head banner that marked it as the ship of Diomedes' heir.

"Can we outrun them?" Heracles asked.

Argus studied the approaching fleet with a sailor's eye and shook his head grimly. "Not loaded as we are, with horses aboard. They'll overhaul us before we're five miles from shore."

The sea battle that followed became legendary among the sailors of both nations. The Greeks, outnumbered and laden with their supernatural cargo, fought with the desperate courage of men who knew death waited in the dark waters below. The Thracians, grief-mad with the loss of their king, pressed their attack with suicidal fury.

Ships rammed and grappled in the choppy seas. Bronze-tipped arrows darkened the sky. Men screamed and died, feeding the waves with their blood. And through it all, the mares of Diomedes stood in their improvised stalls, their eyes reflecting the chaos around them with an intelligence that seemed almost human.

The tide turned when Heracles managed to board the Thracian flagship. His great club swept the deck clear of defenders, and when the enemy captain challenged him to single combat, the son of Zeus ended the duel with a single tremendous blow that drove his opponent clean through the deck planks.

With their leader dead and their flagship disabled, the Thracian fleet broke off the engagement. But the victory had come at terrible cost. Three of their companions lay dead, including brave Lycaon, and the ship was so badly damaged that every man aboard had to take turns with the baling buckets to keep her afloat.

The voyage home took eight days, eight days of constant vigilance as they nursed their wounded vessel across the wine-dark sea. The mares grew quieter as they travelled south, as if the very distance from their cursed homeland was healing them further. By the time they reached Greek waters, they were drinking water instead of blood, though they still refused any grain or hay offered to them.

Eurystheus was waiting at the harbour of Tiryns, surrounded by his usual retinue of guards and courtiers. But when he saw what Heracles had brought him, four horses that still radiated an aura of barely contained violence, his thin face went white with terror.

"Magnificent," he said, though his voice shook. "Truly magnificent. Take them… take them to my stables at once."

But when the grooms approached with their leads and bridles, Podargos reared up on her hind legs, her sharp teeth bared in what might have been a smile. The stablemen scattered like leaves before the wind, and even Eurystheus took several hasty steps backward.

"On second thought," the king said quickly, "perhaps they would be better suited to... to freedom. Yes, release them into the mountains. Let them run wild."

And so the mares of Diomedes were turned loose in the forests of Arcadia, where the mountain wolves were said to hunt in packs large enough to bring down even such terrible prey. Whether the wolves devoured them or they devoured the wolves, none could say. But sometimes, on dark nights when the wind howled through the peaks, shepherds claimed they could hear the sound of galloping hooves and hungry growling echoing from the deepest valleys.

As for Heracles, he returned to his labours with the knowledge that he had done more than simply complete another of Eurystheus' tasks. He had broken a curse, ended a tyrant's reign, and perhaps most importantly, proven that even the darkest monsters could be redeemed if one had the courage to face them directly.

Sigurd's Escape On The Wonderful Horse Gullfaxi

An Icelandic Tale

This tale has been adapted from a story from A. W. Hall's book Icelandic Fairy Tales and Folk Tales, published by Frederick Warne And Co., London, in 1897.

A. W. Hall, often referenced as Mrs. Angus W. Hall, was a translator and editor active in the late 19th and early 20th centuries. She meticulously collected, translated, and adapted these traditional Icelandic folk narratives for English-speaking audiences, aiming to preserve the stories' cultural authenticity while making them accessible and suitable, especially for younger readers.

Sigurd led the beautiful steed, Gullfaxi, outside the castle, and had just mounted, when Helga came running to him with something in her hand.

"Here, I give you a green branch, a stone, and a stick," she said, "else I fear that you may get into trouble. Listen carefully to what I tell you. If, when you are mounted on the horse, an enemy should follow you and threaten to take your life, you have only to throw down the green branch as you ride along, and immediately a dense forest will grow up behind you. Should the enemy still attempt to follow, you have only to strike the stick on the white stone, and a terrible hailstorm will kill all who come after you."

As she finished speaking, and Sigurd gathered up the reins to start off, Helga gave a cry of terror. Striding over the brow of the hill, she saw the huge form of her father.

"Fly! fly!" she said. "Use the steed for your own protection. It is your only chance of life. Save yourself, for my sake."

Raising his cap in farewell to his young hostess, Sigurd set spurs to Gullfaxi, and as the noble animal put forth his full speed, the prince turned in the saddle and shook his fist at the angry giant.

Without staying to question his daughter, the giant strode after his horse and Sigurd, breathing out threats of vengeance. At first he could only just keep them in sight; but, with his gigantic strides, he soon began to gain upon them when the ground grew rocky and hilly. Then Sigurd threw down Helga's green branch, and immediately a thick forest rose between him and his enemy.

But the giant seized his axe, and began with mighty strokes to hew his way through the wood. Crash went trees and bushes; crash, crash, to right and to left, and when Sigurd looked back a second time, the giant was through the forest, and close behind him. Then Sigurd touched the white stone with his stick, and immediately such a terrible hailstorm broke loose behind him that the giant was killed on the spot, while Sigurd rode on in bright sunshine.

With the giant dead, Sigurd thought he would return and fetch Helga, but while he was debating which road to take, he saw his stepmother's dog running towards him. The dog was dusty and footsore, and whined piteously as he drew near. Sigurd dismounted, and went to meet him. The dog put his paws upon the prince's knee, and looked up at him with tears running down his face. Then Sigurd's heart was very heavy, for he knew misfortune was threatening his beloved stepmother. He leapt on to his horse, and rode at full speed, taking no rest, either by day or night, till at length he came out of the thick pinewoods, and saw the palace before him. In the courtyard a great crowd was assembled, and there, fastened to a stake, and surrounded by huge faggots, he saw the graceful figure of his stepmother.

"Here is Sigurd, Sigurd, the king's lost son," he heard voices say, as if in a dream, as he galloped furiously on.

He, however, saw nothing but the beautiful pale face of the queen as he leaped from his horse, and pushed his way through the crowd, sword in hand. He cut the bands with which Injibjörg was fastened, scattered the guards, and carried her into the palace, to his father's room.

There he found the king lying on his couch, sick and near death for grief at the loss of his son.

"My father," Sigurd cried, as he stood before him with his arm round his stepmother, "what is this that has been done? Why has my mother been treated thus in my absence?"

"My son," his father cried, hardly believing that he saw him alive and well before him, "where have you been? The people declared the queen had taken your life, and she was therefore condemned to death, while I was too ill to save her from their vengeance. Forgive me, Sigurd, and beg the queen also to pardon me," and he embraced them both with the utmost affection.

Then Sigurd related all his adventures, and how he had freed Injibjörg for ever from the hateful power of her sisters. His love for his stepmother was greater than ever, as he heard of all that she had suffered in his absence. He was not happy now when she was out of his sight, and he tried in every way to make up to her for what had passed. He told her, too, of Helga in the castle by the lake; and when she was quite restored to health, he set out, with her blessing and that of his father, to fetch the maiden to his home, as he had promised.

Helga was rejoiced to see Sigurd again, for she had watched for him day by day. They brought away all the treasures of the castle, and in a short time there was a magnificent wedding between Helga and Sigurd, the marriage feast lasting a whole month.

When the king died, Sigurd and Helga came to the throne, and, guided by the wise counsels of Injibjörg, the kingdom became renowned far and near for its good rule and the happiness of its people.

The Speaking Horse

A Sri Lankan Tale

This tale is my version of an original tale by Henry Parker in his book, Village Folk-Tales of Ceylon, Volume 1, published by Luzac And Co., London, in 1910. This tale was related to Henry Parker by E. G. Goonewardene, Esq., of the North-western Province.

Henry Parker was a British civil servant and folklorist who worked in colonial Sri Lanka (then Ceylon) during the late 19th and early 20th centuries. Deeply interested in the island's culture, Parker collected and translated a wealth of Sinhalese folklore, legends, and village beliefs, preserving them in English for a wider audience. His most notable work, Village Folk-Tales of Ceylon (1890–1910), is a three-volume collection that remains a significant resource on South Asian oral traditions.

There was once a certain King who was greatly wanting in common sense, and in his kingdom there was a Panditaya who was extremely wise. The King had a very beautiful white horse of which he was very proud. The Panditaya was respected and revered by all, but for the King little or no respect was felt, on account of his foolish conduct. He observed this, and became jealous of the Panditaya's popularity, so he determined to destroy him.

One day he sent for him. The Panditaya came and prostrated himself before the King, who said, "I hear that you are extremely learned and wise. I require you to teach my white horse to speak. I will allow you one week to consider the matter, at the end of which time you must give me a reply, and if you cannot do it your head will be cut off."

The Panditaya replied, "It is good, O Great King," and went home in very low spirits.

He lived with a beautiful daughter, now a grown-up girl. When he returned she observed that he was melancholy, and asked the reason, on which the Panditaya informed her of the King's command, and said that it was impossible to teach a horse to speak, and that he must place his affairs in order, in preparation for his death.

"Do as I tell you," she said, "and your life will be saved. When you go to the King on the appointed day, and he asks you if you are able to teach his horse to speak, you must answer, 'I can do it, but it is a work that will occupy a long time. I shall require seven years' time for it. You must also allow me to keep the horse by me and ride it, while you will provide food for it.' The King will agree to this, and in the meantime who knows what may happen?"

The Panditaya accepted this wise advice. He appeared before the King at the end of the week, and prostrated himself. The

King asked him, "Are you able to teach my white horse to speak?"

"Maharajani," he replied, "I am able." He then explained that it would be a very difficult work, and would occupy a long time, and that he would require seven years for it, and must have the horse by him all the time, and use it, while the King would provide food for it.

The King was delighted at the idea of getting his horse taught to speak, and at once agreed to these conditions. So the Panditaya took away the horse, and kept it at the King's expense.

Before the seven years had elapsed the King had died, and the horse remained with the Panditaya.

The Wings of Chollima

A Korean Tale

This is my own version of a traditional legend, written and adapted from various sources and historical notes in my collection of folk and fairy tales.

Chollima (천리마 / 千里馬, literally "thousand-li horse") is a mythical winged horse said to be so swift that no rider could ever mount it before it flew away. In Korean tradition, the horse symbolises speed, strength, and unyielding spirit. The legend itself has roots in Chinese mythology, namely the "qianlima" (千里马, "thousand-li horse") of ancient Chinese texts, a steed able to travel a thousand li (hundreds of miles) in a single day. When this idea entered Korea, it evolved into the winged horse Chollima, which became a distinctly Korean cultural symbol.

Long ago, when the mountains of Korea still spoke to the clouds and tigers roamed beneath the pines, there lived a young farmer named Min-joon, who worked the poorest plot of land in the village of Cheongmae.

Min-joon had inherited a barren stretch of earth, filled with stones and sorrow, from his father who had died during the last harvest. Though his neighbours pitied him, none offered help, for his land was said to be cursed, and no seeds dared to sprout in its dry, cracked soil.

But Min-joon worked anyway. Each morning, before the sun had climbed over the hills, he hoisted his wooden hoe and dug. He dug through rock, through frost, through despair. He toiled with such quiet resolve that even the trees bent to watch.

One day, as spring tried to chase the last snow from the valleys, Min-joon discovered something strange: a single white feather, lodged between the stones. It shimmered like morning mist and pulsed faintly with warmth.

That night, he dreamt of a great horse with wings like a crane, its hooves never touching the ground. It looked at him with eyes deeper than oceans and said only, "If you chase me, I will fly. If you doubt me, I will vanish. But if you believe, I will carry you beyond what is known."

Min-joon awoke with a start. The feather was still in his hand.

From that day on, whenever he went to till the field, he would hear a distant thunder, yet the skies were clear. And sometimes, in the corner of his eye, he saw a blur of white, galloping just beyond the trees.

"It is Chollima," whispered the village elder when Min-joon shared what he had seen. "The flying horse. He comes only to those who do not yield to hardship. But beware, for he can never be caught. Not even the strongest king has laid a hand on his mane."

"But what does he want with me?" Min-joon asked.

"Perhaps he sees something in you. Or perhaps he is only testing your legs."

So Min-joon began to run. Every morning, before the fields, he ran through forests, over hills, and across frozen rivers. Every day, Chollima appeared, always just ahead, hooves skimming the ground, mane rippling like moonlight. The horse never spoke again, but Min-joon felt its call like fire in his blood.

One evening, when the plum blossoms fell like snow and the moon hung low over the hills, Min-joon came to a cliff above the Lake of Sky Mirrors. There, Chollima stood, waiting.

"I've run as far as my legs can carry me," Min-joon gasped.

The horse stepped forward, silent. Its wings shimmered.

Then it turned and leapt from the cliff.

Min-joon's heart stopped. He ran to the edge, looking down but saw nothing other than the reflection of stars in the still water of the lake.

With a sad heart he turned to leave, but then paused. The feather. He still carried it, always tucked in his sleeve. It now glowed faintly. He closed his eyes. And then he jumped.

The wind screamed past his face, but then it suddenly lifted. Beneath him, wings unfolded like clouds parting for the moon. He was no longer falling. He was flying.

Min-joon looked down to see Chollima beneath him, its body warm and strong, its wings unfurled like sails of silk. It said nothing. It did not need to.

Together, they soared over mountains, rivers, and the breath of heaven itself. Time lost its endless decay, and fear vanished from Min-Joon's mind.

When they landed, Min-joon stood no longer as a poor farmer, but as a man who had seen the shape of miracles.

Chollima lowered its head and let Min-joon touch its brow. Then, with a cry that split the stars, it vanished into the wind, leaving behind only a single hoofprint in the soil. Where the hoof struck the ground, a spring burst forth, a source of sweet water that never ran dry. Min-joon's land bloomed. Crops grew without seed. Trees bore fruit in winter. His field became the heart of the village, feeding the hungry, and healing the sick.

The Wonderful Horse

A Pawnee Tale

This tale has been adapted from a story from Carrie de Voe's book Legends of The Kaw, published by Franklin Hudson Publishing Co., Kansas, in 1904.

Carrie De Voe was an American folklorist active in the late 19th and early 20th centuries, known for collecting and publishing regional folklore, particularly from the American Midwest and Missouri. Her work focused on preserving oral traditions, local legends, and ghost stories, often with a particular interest in supernatural and frontier themes.

An old woman lived on the outskirts of a village located on the bank of the Platte River. At one time she had been the wife of a brave hunter and warrior. During his life there was always a comfortable lodge, as well as plenty of buffalo meat and robes. No one of the nation was more successful in stealing horses from the enemy, which was considered a highly honourable feat. He was killed in a great battle with the Sioux, and the poor woman had never ceased to mourn. Now, in old age, there remained but one relative, a grandson of sixteen years. Being reduced to poverty, they were in the habit, when the tribe moved, of following in the rear, in order to pick up anything that might have been left behind as worthless. Once, to the delight of the boy, an old dun horse was abandoned by its owner. The animal was blind in one eye and had a sore back and a swollen leg, but was nevertheless valuable to the poor woman, inasmuch as it could carry the cooking utensils and the worn-out skin used for a lodge when traveling.

The village was moved to Court House Rock. Soon after arrival the young men sent out to look for buffaloes returned with information that there was a large herd in the vicinity, and among the animals was a spotted calf.

The head chief had a young and beautiful daughter. He announced that whosoever should kill the spotted calf should marry the girl. Since the buffaloes were only four miles away, it was decided that the charge should be made from the village. The one who had the fastest steed would be most likely to obtain the calf. The poor boy made preparations to ride the old dun horse, but he was ridiculed to such an extent that he withdrew to the bank of a creek, nearby.

There the animal turned its head and said, "Plaster me all over with mud. Cover my head, neck, body and legs."

The boy obeyed and the horse then ordered that he remain where they were and make the charge from the creek. The men were drawn up in line and at the word *Loo ah* (go), leaned forward, yelled and galloped away. At one side, some distance away, the dun horse flew over the ground. Strangely, he suddenly seemed young and strong of limb and sure of foot. As they neared the buffaloes, he dashed in among the herd and stopped beside the spotted calf. His rider killed it, and taking another arrow, shot a fat cow, then dismounting, secured the spotted skin. Cutting out certain portions of the meat, the boy packed them upon the horse. Putting the skin on top of the load, he led the animal back to camp. It pranced and curveted and showed much spirit. The warriors were filled with astonishment. A rich chief rode up to the boy and tried to buy the spotted robe, but without success.

Some of the hunters reached the village in advance and informed the old woman of her grandson's triumph. She could hardly believe the story, and wondered if they were still ridiculing her boy. His appearance with the coveted robe and more meat than they had had for many a long day, ended her doubts, and there were great rejoicings in the tent.

At night the horse spoke to the boy, saying, "Tomorrow the Sioux are coming. There will be a battle. When they are drawn up in line, jump on me and ride as hard as you can up to the head chief and kill him and ride back. Ride up to them four times and kill four of the bravest Sioux, but do not go the fifth time or you will get killed or lose me."

The next morning, just around day-break, the Sioux rode over the top of the hill and drew up in line of battle. They were attired in all the trappings of war, and looked ferocious in their paint. The Pawnees had no time for decoration, but hastily seized their weapons, cut the lariats that bound their ponies, sprang upon them and rushed out of the camp. When they reached the proper distance, they formed themselves in battle array opposite the enemy.

It was the custom of these tribes, when ready for a fight, to confront one another in two long lines. After a few moments of silence, some man, desiring to distinguish himself, rode out from the attacking party and exhorted his people, telling them of brave deeds in the past and of what he now intended to do. Then, turning quickly, he dashed toward the enemy, hanging over the side of his pony and riding along in front of the foe, discharging one arrow after another, in rapid succession. If the brave were killed, his own people made no sign, until a man rode out from the other side to challenge. If he were fiercely set upon, they united in a general attack.

The boy mounted the dun horse and joined the warriors. They looked askance but were too excited to make comment. The wonderful horse galloped out from the line and made for the head chief of the Sioux. The boy quickly despatched the leader and rode back to the Pawnees. Four times he went forward, and each time killed one of the bravest of the enemy. Then, forgetting the warning, the boy charged again. An arrow struck his horse and the rider had a narrow escape from death. The Sioux cut and chopped the horse in pieces.

After a spirited conflict, the Pawnees were victorious. The following day the boy went out to where the horse lay. Gathering up the pieces of flesh, he put them in a pile, and wrapping himself in his blanket, sat on the top of a hill not far away. He drew the robe over his head and mourned. A storm arose suddenly. The wind blew and rain fell. Removing the blanket from his face, the boy saw the pieces coming together and taking form. Another storm came, and when it cleared away, he beheld a slight movement of the horse's tail. Then the animal lifted its head from the ground. After a fourth storm had spent its fury, the horse arose and its owner hastened down the hill and led it home. It cautioned him to render perfect obedience in the future, and said, "Lead me away from the camp, behind that hill. Leave me there tonight and come for me in the morning."

The boy did as directed, and found, standing beside his old friend, a beautiful white horse.

Leaving the dun horse a second night, the owner discovered a fine black gelding in the morning. After ten nights, there were ten horses, each of a different colour. The boy was now rich and married the daughter of the chief. Many years later he became the head of the nation. The old grandmother was well cared for, and the dun horse, being considered sacred, was never mounted except at a doctor's dance, but was led around with the chief wherever he went.

The Magician's Horse

A Hungarian Tale

This story has been adapted from a tale told by Andrew Lang in The Grey Fairy Book, which was originally published by Longmans, Green And Co., London & New York, in 1900.

Andrew Lang (1844–1912) was a Scottish poet, novelist, literary critic, and folklorist best known for his influential work in collecting and popularizing folk and fairy tales from around the world. While Lang often served as editor and commentator, much of the translation and collection work was done by his wife, Leonora Blanche Alleyne. Lang's writings helped revive interest in folklore and mythology during the Victorian era and laid a foundation for modern comparative folklore studies.

Once upon a time, there was a king who had three sons. Now it happened that one day the three princes went out hunting in a large forest at some distance from their father's palace, and the youngest prince lost his way, so his brothers had to return home without him.

For four days the prince wandered through the glades of the forest, sleeping on moss beneath the stars at night, and by day living on roots and wild berries. At last, on the morning of the fifth day, he came to a large open space in the middle of the forest, and here stood a stately palace, but neither within nor without was there a trace of human life. The prince entered the open door and wandered through the deserted rooms without seeing a living soul.

At last he came on a great hall, and in the centre of the hall was a table spread with dainty dishes and choice wines. The prince sat down, and satisfied his hunger and thirst, and immediately afterwards the table disappeared from his sight. This struck the prince as very strange; but though he continued his search through all the rooms, upstairs and down, he could find no one to speak to. At last, just as it was beginning to get dark, he heard steps in the distance and he saw an old man coming towards him up the stairs.

"What are you doing wandering about my castle?" asked the old man.

The prince replied, "I lost my way hunting in the forest. If you will take me into your service, I should like to stay with you, and will serve you faithfully."

"Very well," said the old man. "You may enter my service. You will have to keep the stove always lit, you will have to fetch the wood for it from the forest, and you will have the charge of the black horse in the stables. I will pay you a florin a day, and at mealtimes you will always find the table in the hall spread with food and wine, and you can eat and drink as much as you require."

The prince was satisfied, and he entered the old man's service, and promised to see that there was always wood on the stove, so that the fire should never die out. Now, though he did not know it, his new master was a magician, and the flame of the stove was a magic fire, and if it had gone out the magician would have lost a great part of his power.

One day the prince forgot, and let the fire burn so low that it very nearly burnt out. Just as the flame was flickering the old man stormed into the room.

"What do you mean by letting the fire burn so low?" he growled. "I have only arrived in the nick of time." And while the prince hastily threw a log on the stove and blew on the ashes to kindle the glow, his master gave him a severe box on the ear, and warned him that if ever it happened again it would fare badly with him.

One day the prince was sitting disconsolate in the stables when, to his surprise, the black horse spoke to him.

"Come into my stall," it said, "I have something to say to you. Fetch my bridle and saddle from that cupboard and put them on me. Take the bottle that is beside them, for it contains an ointment which will make your hair shine like pure gold. Then put all the wood you can gather together on to the stove, till it is piled quite high up."

So the prince did what the horse told him. He saddled and bridled the horse, he put the ointment on his hair till it shone like gold, and he made such a big fire in the stove that the flames sprang up and set fire to the roof, and in a few minutes the palace was burning like a huge bonfire.

Then he hurried back to the stables, and the horse said to him, "There is one thing more you must do. In the cupboard you will find a looking-glass, a brush and a riding-whip. Bring them with you, mount on my back, and ride as hard as you can, for now the house is burning merrily."

The prince did as the horse bade him. Scarcely had he got into the saddle than the horse was off and away, galloping at such a pace that, in a short time, the forest and all the country belonging to the magician lay far behind them.

In the meantime the magician returned to his palace, which he found in smouldering ruins. In vain he called for his servant. At last he went to look for him in the stables, and when he discovered that the black horse had disappeared too, he at once suspected that they had gone together; so he mounted a roan horse that was in the next stall, and set out in pursuit.

As the prince rode, the quick ears of his horse heard the sound of pursuing feet.

"Look behind you," he said, "and see if the old man is following."

And the prince turned in his saddle and saw a cloud like smoke or dust in the distance.

"We must hurry," said the horse.

After they had galloped for some time, the horse said again, "Look behind, and see if he is still at some distance."

"He is quite close," answered the prince.

"Then throw the looking-glass on the ground," said the horse. So the prince threw it, and when the magician came up, the roan horse stepped on the mirror, and crash, his foot went through the glass, and he stumbled and fell, cutting his feet so badly that there was nothing for the old man to do but to go slowly back with him to the stables, and put new shoes on his feet. Then they started once more in pursuit of the prince, for the magician set great value on the horse, and was determined not to lose it.

In the meanwhile the prince had gone a great distance, but the quick ears of the black horse detected the sound of following feet from afar.

"Dismount," he said to the prince. "Put your ear to the ground, and tell me if you do not hear a sound."

So the prince dismounted and listened. "I seem to hear the earth tremble," he said. "I think he cannot be very far off."

"Mount me at once," answered the horse, "and I will gallop as fast as I can." And he set off so fast that the earth seemed to fly from under his hoofs.

"Look back once more," he said, after a short time, "and see if he is in sight."

"I see a cloud and a flame," answered the prince, "but a long way off."

"We must make haste," said the horse. And shortly after he said, "Look back again, for he can't be far off now."

The prince turned in his saddle, and exclaimed, "He is close behind us, in a minute the flame from his horse's nostrils will reach us."

"Then throw the brush on the ground," said the horse.

And the prince threw it, and in an instant the brush was changed into such a thick wood that even a bird could not have got through it, and when the old man got up to it the roan horse came suddenly to a stand-still, not able to advance a step into the thick tangle. So there was nothing for the magician to do but to retrace his steps, to fetch an axe, with which he cut himself a way through the wood. But it took him some time, during which the prince and the black horse got on well ahead.

But once more they heard the sound of pursuing feet. "Look back," said the black horse, "and see if he is following."

"Yes," answered the prince, "this time I hear him distinctly."

"Let us hurry on," said the horse. And a little later he said, "Look back now, and see if he is in sight."

"Yes," said the prince, turning round, "I see the flame. He is close behind us."

"Then you must throw down the whip," answered the horse. And in the twinkling of an eye the whip was changed into a broad river. When the old man got up to it he urged the roan horse into the water, but as the water mounted higher and higher, the magic flame which gave the magician all his power grew smaller and smaller, till, with a fizz, it went out, and the old man and the roan horse sank in the river and disappeared. When the prince looked round they were no longer to be seen.

"Now," said the horse, "you may dismount. There is nothing more to fear, for the magician is dead. Beside that brook you will find a willow wand. Gather it, and strike the earth with it, and it will open and you will see a door at your feet."

When the prince struck the earth with the wand a door appeared, and opened into a large, vaulted stone hall.

"Lead me into that hall," said the horse, "I will stay there, but you must go through the fields till you reach a garden, in the midst of which is a king's palace. When you get there you must ask to be taken into the king's service. Good-bye, and don't forget me."

So they parted, but first the horse made the prince promise not to let anyone in the palace see his golden hair. So he bound a scarf round it, like a turban, and the prince set out through the fields, till he reached a beautiful garden, and beyond the garden he saw the walls and towers of a stately palace. At the garden gate he met the gardener, who asked him what he wanted.

"I want to take service with the king," replied the prince.

"Well, you may stay and work under me in the garden," said the man, for as the prince was dressed like a poor man, he could not tell that he was a king's son. "I need someone to weed the ground and to sweep the dead leaves from the paths. You shall have a florin a day, a horse to help you to cart the leaves away, and food and drink."

So the prince consented, and set about his work. But when his food was given to him he only ate half of it; the rest he carried to the vaulted hall beside the brook, and gave to the black horse. And this he did every day, and the horse thanked him for his faithful friendship.

One evening, as they were together, after his work in the garden was over, the horse said to him, "Tomorrow a large company of princes and great lords are coming to your king's palace. They are coming from far and near, as wooers for the three princesses. They will all stand in a row in the courtyard of the palace, and the three princesses will come out, and each will carry a diamond apple in her hand, which she will throw into the air. At whosoever's feet the apple falls, well, he will be the bridegroom of that princess. You must be close by in the garden at your work. The apple of the youngest princess, who is much the most beautiful of the sisters, will roll past the wooers and stop in front of you. Pick it up at once and put it in your pocket."

The next day, when the wooers were all assembled in the courtyard of the castle, everything happened just as the horse had said. The princesses threw the apples into the air, and the diamond apple of the youngest princess rolled past all the wooers, out on to the garden, and stopped at the feet of the young gardener, who was busy sweeping the leaves away. In a moment he had stooped down, picked up the apple and put it in his pocket. As he stooped the scarf round his head slipped a little to one side, and the princess caught sight of his golden hair, and loved him from that moment.

The king was very sad, for his youngest daughter was the one he loved best, but there was no help for it, and the next day a threefold wedding was celebrated at the palace, and after the wedding the youngest princess returned with her husband to the small hut in the garden where he lived.

Sometime after this the people of a neighbouring country went to war with the king, and he set out to battle, accompanied by the husbands of his two eldest daughters mounted on stately steeds. But the husband of the youngest daughter had nothing but the old broken-down horse which helped him in his garden work, and the king, who was ashamed of this son-in-law, refused to give him any other.

So, as he was determined not to be left behind, he went into the garden, mounted the sorry nag, and set out. But scarcely had he ridden a few yards before the horse stumbled and fell. So he dismounted and went down to the brook, to where the black horse lived in the vaulted hall. And the horse said to him, "Saddle and bridle me, and then go into the next room and you will find a suit of armour and a sword. Put them on, and we will ride forth together to battle."

And the prince did as he was told, and when he had mounted the horse his armour glittered in the sun, and he looked so brave and handsome, that no one would have recognised him as the gardener who swept away the dead leaves from the paths. The horse bore him away at a great pace, and when they reached the battle-field they saw that the king was losing the day, and so many of his warriors had been slain. But when the warrior on his black charger and in glittering armour appeared on the scene, hewing right and left with his sword, the enemy were dismayed and fled in all directions, leaving the king master of the field.

Then the king and his two sons-in-law, when they saw their deliverer, shouted, and all that was left of the army joined in the cry. "A god has come to our rescue!" And they would have surrounded him, but his black horse rose in the air and bore him out of their sight.

Soon after this, part of the country rose in rebellion against the king, and once more he and his two sons-in-law had to fare forth to battle. And the son-in-law who was disguised as a gardener wanted to fight too. So he came to the king and said, "Dear father, let me ride with you to fight your enemies."

"I don't want a blockhead like you to fight for me," answered the king. "Besides, I haven't got a horse fit for you. But see, there is a carter on the road carting hay, you may take his horse."

So the prince took the carter's horse, but the poor beast was old and tired, and after it had gone a few yards it stumbled and fell. So the prince returned sadly to the garden and watched the king ride forth at the head of the army accompanied by his two sons-in-law. When they were out of sight the prince betook himself to the vaulted chamber by the brook-side, and having taken counsel of the faithful black horse, he put on the glittering suit of armour, and was borne on the back of the horse through the air, to where the battle was being fought. And once more he routed the king's enemies, hacking to right and left with his sword. And again they all cried. "A god has come to our rescue!" But when they tried to detain him the black horse rose in the air and bore him out of their sight.

When the king and his sons-in-law returned home they could talk of nothing but the hero who had fought for them, and all wondered who he could be.

Shortly afterwards the king of a neighbouring country declared war, and once more the king and his sons-in-law and his subjects had to prepare themselves for battle, and once more the prince begged to ride with them, but the king said he had no horse to spare for him. "But," he added, "you may take the horse of the woodman who brings the wood from the forest, it is good enough for you."

So the prince took the woodman's horse, but it was so old and useless that it could not carry him beyond the castle gates. So he took himself once more to the vaulted hall, where the black horse had prepared a still more magnificent suit of armour for him than the one he had worn on the previous occasions, and when he had put it on, and mounted on the back of the horse, he bore him straight to the battle-field, and once more he scattered the king's enemies, fighting single-handed in their ranks, and they fled in all directions.

But it happened that one of the enemy struck with his sword and wounded the prince in the leg. And the king took his own pocket-handkerchief, with his name and crown embroidered on it, and bound it round the wounded leg. And the king would have compelled him to mount in a litter and be carried straight to the palace, while two of his knights were to lead the black charger to the royal stables. But the prince put his hand on the mane of his faithful horse, and managed to pull himself up into the saddle, and the horse mounted into the air with him. Then they all shouted and cried, "The warrior who has fought for us is a god! He must be a god."

And throughout all the kingdom nothing else was spoken about, and all the people said, "Who can the hero be who has fought for us in so many battles? He cannot be a man, he must be a god."

And the king said, "If only I could see him once more, and if it turned out that after all he was a man and not a god, I would reward him with half my kingdom."

Now when the prince reached his home, the gardener's hut where he lived with his wife. he was weary, and he lay down on his bed and slept. His wife noticed the handkerchief bound round his wounded leg, and she wondered what it could be. Then she looked at it more closely and saw in the corner that it was embroidered with her father's name and the royal crown. So she ran straight to the palace and told her father. And he and his two sons-in-law followed her back to her house, and there the gardener lay asleep on his bed. And the scarf that he always wore bound round his head had slipped off, and his golden hair gleamed on the pillow. And they all recognised that this was the hero who had fought and won so many battles for them.

Then there was great rejoicing throughout the land, and the king rewarded his son-in-law with half of his kingdom, and he and his wife reigned happily over it.

The Peasant And The Horse

A Russian Tale

This is my version of a tale told by Kate Douglas Wiggin and Nora Archibald Smith in their book, The Talking Beasts, published by Houghton Mifflin Company, New York & Boston, in 1911.

This tale is based on an original by Ivan Andreyevich Krylov, a celebrated Russian fabulist, poet, playwright, and folklorist of the late 18th and early 19th centuries. Born in 1769, Krylov became best known for his sharp, satirical fables, which adapted classical formats, particularly those of Aesop and La Fontaine, into the Russian idiom.

Kate Douglas Wiggin (1856–1923) and her sister Nora Archibald Smith (1859–1934) were American authors and educators known for their influential work in children's literature and early childhood education.

Once upon a time, in a quiet village tucked between the pine-clad hills of old Rus', there lived a humble peasant named Mikhail. He was a man of simple habits and deep wisdom, the sort of man who spoke little, worked hard, and watched the world as a tree watches the seasons, patiently and without complaint.

Mikhail owned a small plot of land, a log house with a thatched roof, and a strong young bay horse named Vezhlik, whose lustrous mane shone like brushed copper in the morning sun. Vezhlik was proud and handsome and, like many creatures of youth, full of opinions and empty of understanding.

Now, one bright spring morning, as the birch trees were just beginning to show their green lacework and the storks had returned to their nests, Mikhail hitched his plough and led Vezhlik into the field. The earth was damp and rich from the melting snow, and the crows wheeled overhead, cawing like gossiping old widows.

Mikhail worked steadily, turning the black soil under with care and rhythm, while Vezhlik trotted nearby in his paddock, watching the scene unfold. The peasant's hands sowed golden oats into the furrows with gentle precision.

Vezhlik, who fancied himself a thinker, stamped and snorted at what he saw. "What foolishness is this?" he muttered under his breath. "Oats! Perfectly good oats! Tossed into the dirt, like old straw or rotting leaves. What waste! What madness! And they call men wise."

He shook his head, his mane tossing like flames in the breeze. "If he gave them to me, I would eat them with gratitude. Or even if he stored them in a bin, yes, hoarded them greedily, I could understand that. That, at least, would have purpose. But this? Feeding the earth? Bah! The ground neither chews nor neighs. It has no belly and no mouth. What use is food to mud?"

And so the horse complained, and the wind carried his words to the corners of the field and beyond, to where the old forest listened with knowing silence.

But Mikhail said nothing. He simply sowed the oats, whistling softly, his boots muddy, his thoughts as steady as the sun on his back.

Seasons passed. Summer came, and with it the long golden days, the buzzing of bees, and the ripening of the crop. The field that once looked barren now shimmered with tall, swaying stalks of grain. The same oats Vezhlik had scorned were now multiplied a hundredfold.

Then came the harvest, and Mikhail reaped what he had sown. He bundled the oats, winnowed them with care, and stored them in the granary, humming a quiet prayer of thanks. Winter arrived with its iron frost and ghost-breath winds, and the world turned white and still.

And what did Mikhail do then?

Each morning, as the snow fell soft and deep, he brought a generous portion of those very oats to Vezhlik's stall. He laid them in the wooden trough, along with hay and fresh water, and stroked the horse's neck as he chewed. Vezhlik ate with great satisfaction, not a trace of his earlier complaints remaining in his mind or mouth.

But one evening, as the wind howled outside and the stars blinked like ice, Mikhail leaned against the stable door and said, more to himself than to the horse, "Funny, isn't it? In spring, you called me foolish. You saw the sowing, but not the harvest. You saw the giving, but not the return. You judged the work without waiting for the fruit."

Vezhlik, hearing the old man's voice, paused his chewing. A trace of shame fluttered in his proud heart, but he said nothing, for what could a horse say in the face of such quiet wisdom?

And the years went on. Each spring, Mikhail sowed. Each autumn, he reaped. And each winter, Vezhlik ate the oats he once called wasted. Only the foolish horse expects the oats to appear in his trough without first being buried in the ground.

Epona of the Silver Mane

A Celtic Tale

This is my own version of a traditional legend, written and adapted from various sources and historical notes in my collection of folk and fairy tales.

The figure of Epona, known as the "Great Mare," originates in Gallo-Roman (Celtic) religion, where she served as the goddess and protector of horses, ponies, donkeys, and mules, a deity unique in her broad appeal. From the first to third centuries AD, her cult was widespread across the Roman Empire, an unusual honour for a Celtic goddess, especially among Roman cavalry units.

Her name is derived from the Gaulish word for "horse" (ek^w*os), combined with an augmentative suffix, essentially meaning "Great Mare".*

Long ago, when the wild woods of Gaul grew thick and strong, and the rivers still remembered the birth of the world, there was a village at the edge of all things. Nestled between thick forests and wide meadows, the people of Branewyn were simple folk, farmers, herders, and horse-breeders known far and wide for their fine steeds. But none was finer than the silver mare called Tarranwyn.

She was a creature of wonder, tall and fleet, with eyes like jet and a mane that shimmered like sunlight on the river's skin. She belonged to no one, yet served the village all the same. At harvest, she pulled the great carts of barley. In times of war, she bore the brave. And in times of peace, she wandered freely from house to house, neighing softly, touching her muzzle to the brows of sleeping babes, as if to bless them.

But as years passed, dark times came. The fields turned cold, the cattle grew sick, and the horses born were dull of eye and weak of limb. The villagers began to whisper: "The gods have turned their backs. We must seek favour again."

An elder woman, Bryneth, as old as moss and as sharp as a hawk's claw, spoke up. "We have forgotten the Horse-Mother, the One who once ran through the sky with stars in her mane. We have forgotten Epona."

The villagers, ashamed, asked, "What must we do?"

Bryneth raised her withered hand. "Each year, we gave a gift to Epona, bread, honey, a carved stone depicting the finest horses, and we set it upon her shrine beneath the standing stone by the river. But the stone was toppled in the last flood, and no one here has thought to raise it again. We must go there. We must seek her."

So, under a full moon, they gathered with bread and honey, with garlands and carvings. Tarranwyn, the silver mare, was led at the front, and when they came to the fallen shrine, she stamped the earth three times. A wind rose, wild and sudden, and the stone rolled back to standing.

Then, before their eyes, Tarranwyn reared up and was no longer a mare, but a woman cloaked in starlight, her hair flowing silver, her hands bare but strong. Around her, the air shimmered with the shapes of white mares and black stallions, galloping as if in a thick mist. She stood barefoot in the grass, tall and radiant, and the villagers fell to their knees.

"I am Epona," she said, her voice both thunder and whisper. "You have called, and I have come. Long have I wandered, forgotten by men. But your love returns me to your hearth."

The people wept, and Bryneth bowed deepest of all. "Forgive us, Lady of the Hoof and Wind."

Epona smiled. "I ask no punishment. I ask only this… respect the herd, honour the wild, and never break a foal's will. Let your daughters ride, let your sons listen to the winds. I will bless you with strength and swiftness, so long as my name is spoken."

And then, as quickly as she had come, Epona became mist, and Tarranwyn stood again among them, breathing slow and calm.

From that day on, the village prospered. The fields grew rich, the foals were born strong, and horses ran with joy across the meadows. Each year, on the night of the full moon, the people laid offerings by the river's stone, and sometimes, just sometimes, children would see a woman with silver hair riding beside the stars.

The Goat And The Horse

A Spanish Tale

This is my own version of a tale written originally as verse by Tomás de Iriarte in his book Literary Fables of Yriarte, published by Ticknor And Fields, London, in 1855.

His most famous collection, Fábulas literarias (1782), offered satirical commentary on literary and social vices, cleverly disguised as stories about animals and allegorical figures. Unlike traditional fables that often focused on simple moral lessons, Iriarte's fables frequently critiqued pedantry, bad writing, and the pretensions of intellectuals, making them both entertaining and intellectually sharp.

It was a warm afternoon in early spring, and the sounds of a traveling fiddler's music drifted through the open meadows like birdsong poured from a bottle. The hills were quiet, save for the occasional hum of insects and the sweet, winding strains of the violin echoing off the tree trunks and stone fences.

At the edge of the pasture, a goat stood unusually still for such a fidgety creature. His head was lifted, ears pricked forward, eyes half-closed in something like reverence. The music stirred something in him he couldn't name, a soft trembling in his hooves, a rhythm his body obeyed without thought. He danced, though he didn't know he danced, each tap of his foot a small salute to the beauty in the air.

A few paces away, tethered loosely under a tree, an old bay horse had also gone still. He had been chewing lazily at a patch of grass when the music caught him, and now his jaw hung slack, the stems forgotten. His long face, so often patient and dull, bore a flicker of memory, something faraway and fine, like sunlight on the surface of a forgotten river.

The goat, overcome with both the joy of the moment and a sudden spurt of strange wisdom, turned toward the horse and said, "Is it not marvellous, friend? That such harmony should come from the strings of a violin?"

The horse said nothing, his eyes still distant.

"The sound," the goat went on, lowering his voice to something reverent, "it comes from the entrails of a goat. One of my kind. He once grazed alongside me, perhaps. We butted horns. We shared salt licks. And now, now his insides sing."

The goat's tone shifted, tinged with pride and something close to envy. "I can only hope that, one day, when my time comes, my body too might give rise to such music. What better purpose, after all, than to bring such sweetness into the world?"

For a long moment, the horse said nothing. Then he turned, slowly and heavily, his great brown eyes settling on the goat with something between amusement and pity.

"Ah," he said at last, "you speak of the strings. Yes. They sing because they are stretched and scraped and drawn taut until they cry out in harmony."

He swished his tail once, thoughtfully. "But the bow, the thing that brings them to life, that's made from hair. My hair, in fact."

The goat blinked, uncertain.

The horse shifted his weight and continued, more gently now. "It was taken long ago, a handful from my tail. I was frightened, at first. And it hurt. But the pain passed. And now, here I stand, listening to that same music you admire, knowing I had a part in it. Small, perhaps, but real. The pleasure is mine, now, in life."

He paused and looked toward the violinist on the hill. "You, my friend, dream of music born from your insides, but such a gift can only be given in death. You may take comfort in your hope, but you'll never hear the song it creates."

The goat stood silent, his hooves still at last. The music played on.

The Black Horse

An Irish Tale

This tale is adapted from a story in Joseph Jacobs' book More Celtic Fairy Tales, published by David Nutt, London, in 1895.

Joseph Jacobs (1854–1916) was an English folklorist, historian, and literary critic best known for collecting and publishing some of the most enduring fairy tales in the English-speaking world. Born in Australia and educated in England, Jacobs sought to preserve and promote traditional English folk narratives at a time when much attention was being paid to continental European tales.

Once upon a time, in an old kingdom, there lived a king who had three sons. When the king died, his lands and treasures were divided between the two eldest sons. But the youngest was left with nothing but a lame, old, white horse.

"If this is all I get," the youngest prince said, "then I suppose I'd better take it and go."

And so he did. Sometimes he rode the limping white horse, sometimes he walked beside it. One day, while traveling across a wide plain, he stopped to let the poor beast graze. As he stood there, a lone rider approached from the west, tall in the saddle, riding fast and skilfully. "All hail, young man," said the stranger.

"Hail to you," said the prince. "What's the news?"

"Only that I'm about ready to break my back riding this beast of a horse," said the man, dismounting. "But tell you what, would you trade that old white nag of yours for mine?"

"No," said the prince. "I'd be worse off than I am now."

"You may think so," said the stranger, "but this black horse here has one gift. There isn't a place in the world he can't carry you to."

So the prince agreed, traded the white garron for the black steed, and climbed into the saddle. He had barely thought about where to go when he found himself, just like that, in the Realm Under the Waves.

There, the Prince of the Underwaves was holding court. The people had gathered to see if anyone was brave or clever enough to go fetch the daughter of the King of the Greeks, to become the prince's bride. No one volunteered, until the newcomer rode up on his black horse.

"You there!" cried the Underwaves prince. "I bind you by spell and vow, bring me the daughter of the King of the Greeks before tomorrow's sunrise!"

The prince went out and leaned his elbow on his horse's neck with a heavy sigh.

"That's the sigh of a prince under a spell," said the black horse. "But worry not, we can do it."

And off they went.

As they neared the great city of the Greeks, the horse said, "No horse has ever entered here before. The princess will see me from her window and want to ride me. Let her, but insist that no one may ride in front of her on this horse except you."

They arrived, and the black horse danced and leapt with such beauty that the princess, watching from above, rushed outside. "Let me ride your horse!" she said.

"You may," said the prince, "but the horse won't allow any man to ride before a lady, only me."

"My own rider will do," she replied.

But when her horseman tried to mount, the black horse kicked him off.

"Then you come ride with me," she said to the prince.

He climbed on, and she climbed behind him. Before she could even catch her breath, the world turned upside down, and in an instant, they were back in the Realm Under the Waves, just as the sun was rising.

"You've returned," said the Underwaves prince.

"I have," said the rider.

"Well done! You're a king's son, but I am a son of fortune. Now let's have the wedding!"

"Not so fast," said the princess. "I won't marry without the silver cup my grandmother and mother both had at their weddings."

"You," said the Underwaves prince to the rider, "bring me that cup by sunrise tomorrow."

Once again, the prince sighed into his horse's mane.

"That's the sigh of a prince under a spell," said the horse. "Mount and we will get the cup."

They travelled back to Greece, where the king and his court were mourning the missing princess. The cup, the horse said, would be passed around at the feast. "Go in," he told the prince. "Sit quietly among them. Say nothing. When the cup reaches you, take it and come out."

He did just that. The cup reached him, he tucked it under his arm, slipped away, and rode off with the black horse. Before sunrise, he was back in the Underwaves.

"You've returned again," said the prince.

"I have," said the rider.

"Now we'll have the wedding!"

"Not yet," said the princess. "First, I need the silver ring my grandmother and mother wore."

"Then bring it!" the Underwaves prince commanded.

The prince went back to the black horse. "This task," the horse said, "is harder than any before, but we will not fail."

They rode through a mountain of snow, a mountain of ice, and a mountain of fire. Each leap left them barely alive. By the end, the prince could hardly stay in the saddle.

They reached a town where the horse said, "Go to the blacksmith. Have him forge an iron spike for every joint in my body."

The prince returned with the spikes.

"Drive them in," said the horse.

He obeyed, and the horse winced with each one.

"There's a lake ahead," the horse said. "When I enter, it will burn. If the lake goes dark before sunrise, I'll return. If not, I won't."

The horse plunged into the water, and the lake blazed like fire. The prince waited, weeping. The night passed, and the sun began to rise.

Then, just as the light touched the lake, the flames went out and the horse emerged from the water, dragging a single spike behind him, with the silver ring hanging from its point.

He collapsed on the shore.

The prince ran to him, held him close, and kept him warm, and by midday, the horse stood up.

"Mount," he said. "Let's go."

They leapt back across the fire, ice, and snow, and reached the Realm Under the Waves.

"You've returned again," said the prince.

"I have," said the rider.

"This time we'll wed!"

"Not quite," said the princess. "I won't marry unless you build me a castle greater than either your father's or mother's."

"You," said the prince, "make that castle before sunrise."

The rider sighed. "This is the easiest of all."

And at a glance, builders and masons appeared, working through the night. By morning, the castle stood.

The Underwaves prince rubbed his eyes in disbelief.

"It's real," said the rider. "See for yourself."

"Now the wedding!" the prince shouted.

"First let's go see the castle," said the princess.

They all went. It was perfect, except for one thing.

"There's no well," said the prince.

"That can be fixed," said the rider. And it was, seven fathoms deep, and wide enough for feasts.

As they looked down into the well, the princess whispered, "There's one last flaw."

"What flaw?" asked the prince.

"Right there," she said.

As he leaned in to look, she shoved him from behind straight down into the well.

"There," she said. "That man may be a prince, but he did none of what was asked. It's the rider of the black horse who did it all, and if he'll have me, then he will be my husband."

And so they were married.

Three years passed. Only then did the rider remember the black horse. Full of guilt, he ran to where he'd last left him, and found the horse still waiting, just as before.

"Greetings," said the horse. "Looks like you've found someone you like better than me."

"No," said the man. "I only forgot. I'm sorry."

"It doesn't matter now. Draw your sword and cut off my head."

"I couldn't possibly!"

"Do it, or I will."

The man raised his sword and struck. As he cried in grief, he heard a voice behind him.

"All hail, brother-in-law!"

He turned and saw the finest man he'd ever laid eyes on.

"What makes you cry for a horse?" the man asked.

"There was never a creature in the world I loved more."

"Would you take me in his place?" asked the stranger.

"If you were him, I would."

"I am the black horse," he said. "I was cursed long ago. No one could keep or ride me until you. You broke the spell. Now come home with me. Let's hold a wedding in my father's hall."

And so they did.

The Tale of the Kiger Mustang

An American Tale

This is my own version of a more recent story. The "Tale of the Kiger Mustang" does not come from an ancient oral tradition in the same sense as Aesop's fables, Celtic myth, or Norse legend. Instead, it is a modern folk-like story that grew out of the discovery and romanticisation of the Kiger Mustang, a wild horse strain found in southeastern Oregon in the late 20th century.

In 1977, during a Bureau of Land Management (BLM) roundup, a herd of mustangs was discovered in the remote Kiger Gorge of Oregon's Steens Mountains. Genetic testing showed these horses carried direct Iberian markers, tracing them back to the Spanish horses brought to the Americas in the 16th century. This gave rise to their reputation as "living links" to the horses of the Conquistadors.

They say the wind remembers. And if you stand long enough among the red buttes of the Oregon high desert, where the sagebrush whispers and the stars hang low, you might hear his gallop, a thundering rhythm carried on the dust, echoing off canyon walls. That is where the story begins, and where it is still told. It is the legend of the wild one they called Spirit.

He was born in a storm, his coat as golden as prairie light, and his eyes sharp with fire. The old mustang mares said that lightning had struck the ground the night he came into the world, splitting the sky above the Kiger Gorge in two. And they believed that some of that sky-fire lived in the foal's chest.

His mother, Red Feather, was lead mare of the Kiger herd, a small band of wild mustangs whose blood ran true to the old Spanish stock brought by conquistadors centuries ago. They were swift, strong, and as sure-footed as goats on the rimrock. Among them, Spirit, even as a colt, showed a kind of defiance, a hunger for speed, and a refusal to follow when he could lead.

By his second winter, he outran the mountain lions. By his third, he challenged his own sire and won, not out of rage, but out of instinct, for he was meant to lead, and so he did.

He led the herd across the dry gullies, over frozen rivers, and through summer heat that shimmered the air. He found water when there was none, and he stood between danger and the youngest foals. His herd grew strong and fast, and the wind carried word of him from Snake River to Steens Mountain. He was the stallion that no man could touch.

But men always come.

One autumn, the Bureau of Land Management came in trucks and helicopters. They said the range was overgrazed, that the mustangs were too many. To the horses, the scream of machines turned to the thunder of hooves in their panic. The herd ran, dust pluming into the sky, but they were cornered. Trapped.

Spirit reared against the steel fences, eyes wide with disbelief. He fought the gates. He kicked until his hooves bled. He called for his herd, but they were caught too. Soon, they were all loaded into trailers, and hauled to a holding facility near Burns.

Spirit would not eat. He would not rest. He would not allow a saddle near his back. The wranglers called him dangerous and proud. One young volunteer, an Umatilla woman named Maya, saw something else, though.

"He's not broken," she said quietly. "He just remembers what freedom feels like."

They named him Spirit in the ledger. Not because he was tame, but because he was anything but.

Spirit was different from the other mustangs. The Bureau knew it too. His build was rare, high Spanish withers, a dorsal stripe, and zebra-striping on his legs. The Kiger mustang breed, though nearly extinct, was alive in him, ancient and beautiful.

Maya lobbied to keep him from auction. She argued that he was more than a horse, he was heritage. After months of calls and pressure, Spirit was moved to a special reserve in southeast Oregon, near the land he once roamed.

Maya visited often. She brought grain, not to bribe him, but to have the time to listen. She'd sit outside his corral for hours, sketching him in her notebook. It was from her sketches that an animator passing through Burns on a research trip took notice. A story was born from the flick of Spirit's ears, and from the steel in his gaze.

They made a film. They called it *Spirit: Stallion of the Cimarron*. The horse on screen became a symbol for wildness, for resistance, for the living memory of the untamed West.

But the real Spirit never bowed his head.

One night, during a storm not unlike the one he was born in, a gate failed. Whether it was rust or wind or will, no one knows, but by morning, the stallion was gone. There were no hoofprints, nor any trail. All they found was the wind and the empty corral.

Some say he returned to the wild, back to the herd he had once led. Others say he was never meant to live behind a fence, that even the earth itself bent for his freedom. And a few folk still ride the rimrock trails and swear, on silent mornings, that they see him, a golden shape against the dawn, mane flying like a banner, a single mustang standing alone on the edge of the sky.

*

In the reserve now, foals are born with the same proud gait, the same fire in their legs. They call them Kigers, and they are watched closely, and protected fiercely. Each carries the echo of that stallion, of Spirit, son of Red Feather, fire of the desert.

Tradition Of The Finding Of Horses

A Ponca Tale

This tale is adapted from a story in Katharine Berry Judson's book Myths and Legends of the Great Plains, published by A. C. McClurg And Co., Chicago, in 1913.

Katherine Berry Judson (1866–1929) was an American historian, folklorist, and educator best known for her influential collections of Indigenous American myths and legends. Working primarily in the early 20th century, she compiled and published numerous volumes of Native American oral traditions.

Long ago, the people followed the Missouri River northward to a place where they could step over the water. Then they turned, and were going across the land. Then they met the Padouca people [Comanche].

At that time the Ponca had no animals but dogs to help them carry burdens. Wherever they went they had to go on foot, but the people were strong and fleet. They could run a great distance and not be weary. One day when they were hunting buffalo, they met the Padouca, and they had many battles with them. The Padouca were mounted on strange animals. At first the Ponca thought it was all one animal.

The Padouca had bows made from elk horn. They were not very long, nor were they very strong. They boiled the horn until it was soft, and then they scraped it, and bound it together with sinews and glue. Their arrows were tipped with bone. They fought also with a stone battle-ax. The handle was a sapling, with a grooved stone axe head, pointed at both ends, which was fastened to this with rawhides.

So the Padouca were terrible fighters. They protected their horses with a covering of thick rawhide cut in round pieces, and put together like fish scales. They spread glue over the outside and then sand. So when the Padouca fought, the arrows of their enemies glanced off the horses' armour. Then the Padouca made breastplates for themselves like those of the horses.

When the Ponca met these terrible warriors, they were afraid. They thought man and horse were one. They named it "Kawa" because they noticed the odour of the horse. Then they knew by this odour when the Padouca were coming. When a man smelled the horses, he would run to the camp and say, "The wind tells us the Kawa are coming."

Then the Ponca would make ready to defend themselves. The Ponca had many battles with the Padouca. They did not know how to use the animals, so they killed the horses as well as the men. Neither could they find out where the Padouca lived.

One day the two tribes had a great battle. The people fought all day. Sometimes the Ponca were driven back, sometimes the Padouca. Then at last a Ponca shot a Padouca so that he fell from his horse. Then the battle ceased. After this, one of the Padouca came toward the Ponca and said in plain Ponca, "Who are you? What do you call yourselves?"

The Ponca replied, "We call ourselves Ponca. You speak our language, are you of our tribe?"

The other said, "No. I speak your language as a gift from a Ponca spirit. One day I lay on a Ponca grave after a battle. Then a man rose from the grave and spoke to me. So I know your language."

Then it was agreed to make peace. The tribes visited each other, and the Ponca traded their bows and arrows for horses. They knew where the Padouca lived. Then the Padouca taught the Ponca how to ride, and how to put burdens on the horses.

When the Ponca had learned how to ride, and had horses, they went to war again. They attacked the Padouca in their own village. They attacked them so many times and stole so many of their horses that at last the Padouca fled. We do not know where they went. The Ponca followed the Platte River toward the rising sun. Then they came back to the Missouri, and they brought their horses with them.

Brother Fox Catches Mr Horse

An American Folktale

This tale is adapted from a story in Joel Chandler Harris' book Nights With Uncle Remus, published by Houghton Mifflin Company, New York & Boston, in 1883.

Joel Chandler Harris (1848–1908) was an American journalist, fiction writer, and folklorist best known for his Uncle Remus stories, a series of African American folktales, fables, and animal stories framed within the character of a kindly, storytelling former slave. Working during the post-Reconstruction era, Harris collected oral tales, many rooted in African, Cherokee, and Southern storytelling traditions, and adapted them into written form using dialect and framed narratives.

"Now this here reminds me of the time Br'er Rabbit got Br'er Fox into one of the worst messes a critter ever found himself in. I may have told it before, but like I always say, a hoe-cake ain't cooked proper 'til it's flipped a few times."

Uncle Remus chuckled to himself before continuing to tell his story to a young boy.

"After Br'er Fox got done hiding from Mr. Dog and filled his belly again, he said to himself, 'I'll be doggone if I don't settle the score with Br'er Rabbit, even if it takes me a whole month!' You see, Br'er Rabbit had tricked him one too many times.

But Br'er Rabbit got wind of it, and he started thinking hard about how to stay one step ahead. One day, while walking down the road, he saw something odd in the pasture, a great big horse, lying flat on its side.

Br'er Rabbit crept up slowly, wondering if the horse was dead. But then he saw the horse flick its tail, and he knew it was just sleeping.

So Br'er Rabbit turned right around and headed back to the road. And who should come trotting along but Br'er Fox?

Br'er Rabbit ran up, calling out, 'Br'er Fox! Oh, Br'er Fox! Come quick! I've got good news for you!'

Now Br'er Fox thought this might be the perfect chance to grab Br'er Rabbit once and for all, so he came hurrying over.

'What's the news?' he asked.

'I've found something,' said Br'er Rabbit. 'A fresh pile of meat, enough to last you all the way through next year!'

Br'er Fox's eyes got wide. 'Where?'

'Over in that pasture. It's a whole horse, lying down. You and me could tie him up and have meat for months.'

Well, Br'er Fox was all in for that. So off they went, and sure enough, there was the horse, still laying in the sun, fast asleep.

But now they had a problem. How were they going to tie the horse down? They started arguing. One had this idea, the other had that. Finally, Br'er Rabbit said, 'I got it. Br'er Fox, you're bigger than me. The only way is for you to let me tie you to the horse's tail. That way, when he gets up, you can hold him down.'

Br'er Fox was a little nervous about this plan, but he didn't want to look scared in front of Br'er Rabbit. So he agreed.

Br'er Rabbit tied him up real tight to that horse's tail. Then he stepped back, hands on his hips, and grinned.

'Well now,' he said, 'if a horse was ever caught, we've caught this one. Looks like we might've tied the bridle on the wrong end, but I reckon you've got the strength to hold him down.'

Then Br'er Rabbit went and found a long switch, trimmed it nice, and gave the horse a good whack!

Whap!

That horse woke up with a start, jumped to his feet, and there went Br'er Fox, dangling behind him like laundry in the wind!

Br'er Rabbit darted out of the way, hollering, 'Hold him down, Br'er Fox! Hold him down! I'll stay right here and make sure everything's fair!'

The horse felt something strange pulling at his tail and figured something was after him. He kicked and bucked and reared and twisted, dragging Br'er Fox every which way.

And Br'er Rabbit just kept jumping around, shouting, 'You got him now! Don't let go! Hold him down, Br'er Fox!'

The horse was bouncing so wild that Br'er Fox looked like a rag caught in a storm. He tried to yell back, 'How'm I supposed to hold him down if I can't even get my feet on the ground?'

But Br'er Rabbit only shouted louder, 'Hold him down! You got him good! Just hold on tight!'

Then the horse kicked, BAM, right in Br'er Fox's stomach, knocking the breath clean out of him.

Another kick came, WHAM, and this time it broke the rope, and sent Br'er Fox flying through the air, spinning like a top.

And Br'er Rabbit just laughed and hollered, 'Hold him down, Br'er Fox!'"

The little boy gasped. "Did Br'er Fox die?"

Uncle Remus shook his head. "Not exactly, honey. But he was real close. All banged up and broken. And while he was laying there healing, it hit him, Br'er Rabbit had fooled him again."

Uncle Remus leaned back in his chair, a chuckle rumbling low in his chest. "Like I always say," he muttered, "you best not go tangling with Br'er Rabbit unless you're ready to be outsmarted."

The Wax Horse

A Sri Lankan Tale

This tale is my version of an original tale by Henry Parker in his book, Village Folk-Tales of Ceylon, Volume 1, published by Luzac And Co., London, in 1910.

Parker approached folklore with both anthropological curiosity and literary care, often providing cultural context or comparative notes alongside the stories. In addition to folktales, he wrote on Sri Lankan archaeology and religious practices, such as in Ancient Ceylon (1909), which covered megalithic culture, demon worship, and ancient irrigation systems.

Long ago, in a distant kingdom, a son was born to a wise and powerful king. As tradition dictated, the king summoned Brahmin astrologers to read the newborn prince's horoscope. After careful study, the Brahmins gave their prediction. When the boy reached adulthood, he would leave his homeland and journey far away, never to return. This troubled the king greatly, and he was determined to stop fate itself.

To prevent this destiny, the king had a chamber built high in the palace towers, secure and luxurious, but carefully guarded. There, the young prince was raised in seclusion, safe from the world and its unpredictable dangers.

As the prince grew, so did his curiosity, and he was allowed amusements, toys, and games to keep him occupied. One day, as he looked out over the bustling street below, he saw a man selling a strange and beautiful toy, a horse made entirely of wax, fitted with delicate wings. It shimmered in the sunlight like something from a dream. Entranced, the prince begged his father to buy it for him.

The king, though cautious, relented. He paid a high price for the wax horse and gave it to his son, unaware that the toy was magical. The horse had the power to fly.

Time passed, and as the prince grew bolder, he discovered how to ride the wax horse through the sky. One night, he slipped away from the tower, mounted the wax horse, and soared off into the dark, star-filled sky, just as the astrologers had foretold.

He flew until he reached a distant kingdom and descended near the home of an elderly woman who sold garlands of flowers to the palace nearby. The prince concealed the wax horse and asked the old flower-seller to let him stay with her. She agreed, and as he stayed there, he learned all he could about the royal family.

Through careful questions, the prince discovered where the king's beautiful daughter, the princess, lived. One night, cloaked in darkness, he mounted the wax horse and flew up to her window. Quiet as a shadow, he entered her chamber, sampled her food and drink, and then vanished before dawn. He returned again and again.

The princess, bewildered by the signs of an invisible visitor, decided to stay awake one night. When the prince entered her chamber, she caught him and, sword in hand, and demanded, "Who are you?"

He introduced himself as a prince from a faraway land. Over time, they grew close and fell in love. He promised to marry her, and for a while, their secret meetings continued.

But soon the princess began to show signs of pregnancy. As was the custom in that kingdom, she was weighed every morning, and the court noticed that her weight was increasing. The king, suspecting foul play, grew furious, and believing that his trusted minister must be to blame, he ordered the man's execution.

The princess's sisters, suspecting the truth, came together to save the innocent minister. They devised a trap. They filled the bathing pool with poisoned perfumed water and posted guards nearby. The next time the prince visited, he went to bathe, as was his habit, and the poison stung his skin. Alarmed and weakened, he rushed to the pool to soothe himself, where the guards captured him.

The prince was dragged before the king. The minister was released, and the king, enraged, ordered the prince to be executed.

As the guards led him away, the prince said calmly, "Please, grant me one final request. There's something I left behind, I'll fetch it and return."

Thinking he was defeated, they allowed him to climb a tree. From among the branches, he pulled out the wax horse he had hidden on his first night in the city. He mounted it, and with a gust of air, soared away to freedom.

That night, he returned again, this time to rescue the princess. Together they fled the city on the flying horse. But as they crossed a wild and tangled forest, the princess, heavily pregnant, was overcome by pain. They landed in a clearing, and the prince left her resting while he went to fetch medicine from a nearby village.

He set the wax horse beside a shop before continuing on foot. But as fate would have it, a fire broke out in the shop next door. The flames leapt toward the wax horse, and before anyone could act, it melted into nothing. The prince was stranded. He tried desperately to return to the princess but could not.

Alone in the wilderness, the princess gave birth to a son. Bitter and abandoned, she left the child behind and wandered away, eventually finding a place among a group of village girls.

Meanwhile, the king, her father, was out hunting in the forest and stumbled upon the crying infant. Touched by the child's innocence, he brought the boy back to the palace and raised him as his own grandson, never knowing the child's true origin.

Years passed, and the boy grew into a handsome and capable young man. When he reached marrying age, he sought a bride, but being of unknown birth, he was turned away by many. One day, while playing, the other boys mocked him, calling him "a foundling." Troubled, he asked the king who raised him about his past and learned the truth, that he had been found in the forest, alone.

Unwilling to let his unknown birth keep him from love, the young man sought a bride among the village girls. Unbeknownst to him, his own mother, now older, quiet, and part of that very group was among them.

Three times he set out to meet the girl he had chosen, and three times he turned back due to strange omens. A hen scolded him one day for stepping on her chicks. Another day, a goat bleated angrily at him for trampling her young. Each time, the animals seemed to sense something unnatural, some cosmic wrong about the marriage he pursued.

At last, on the third day, he pressed forward despite the signs. When he arrived, he met the woman he intended to marry. As they spoke, she told the story of how she had once borne a child in the forest and left him behind.

The truth struck them both like lightning. "Then I must be your son," he said.

Word spread quickly, and the people marvelled at the tale. The young man was reunited with both his mother and, in time, his father, the lost prince, who had never given up searching. Eventually, the young man was crowned king, inheriting the throne from his grandfather, and he ruled with wisdom and justice and married a noblewoman from a royal family. And so, the family that had been scattered by fate and fire was finally made whole again.

The Steed of the Night Journey

An Arabic Tale

This is my own version of a traditional legend, written and adapted from various sources and historical notes in my collection of folk and fairy tales. The Steed of the Night Journey originates from Islamic sacred tradition, specifically the story of the Prophet Muhammad's miraculous journey known as the Isrā' and Mi'rāj.

The tale spread throughout the Islamic world and was retold in both religious commentaries and folk traditions. In some cultures, Burāq is depicted more symbolically, sometimes with a horse's body, wings, and even a human face, embodying a blend of the miraculous and the mystical. The story has been a profound subject in Islamic art, poetry, and storytelling, often emphasizing themes of divine grace, revelation, and the closeness between the human and the divine.

In the hush of ancient Arabia, where the stars drifted across the dunes and moonlight laid silver paths across the sands, there was a moment unlike any other, a moment that tore the veil between Earth and Heaven.

This is the tale of Al-Burāq, the steed born of light and fire, who waited through centuries of stillness for a rider worthy to stir her wings.

Al-Burāq was no ordinary creature. Her body shimmered like polished pearl, and her eyes held the glow of constellations. She stood tall, larger than a mule, but smaller than a horse, and from each of her flanks unfurled wings of flame-shot silk, beating not with wind, but with praise. Her hooves struck no dust, and wherever they touched, the earth turned as soft and as sweet as paradise.

For countless ages, she waited in silence. Though angels offered to ride her, though warriors of heaven sang praises at her side, she waited.

"It is not yet time," she said to herself, her voice a wind through a thousand palms. "I am not born for war. I am not made for glory. I am shaped to carry one heart alone."

The angels nodded, for they too had heard of the one who would journey where no man had gone, from Earth to the Heavens, and beyond.

On a night unlike any other, in the stillest hour, a command spread like lightning through the skies. "Bring the Burāq. The Beloved shall ascend."

The stars trembled with joy. The archangel Jibrīl (Gabriel) descended in radiance and approached Al-Burāq. "It is time," he said.

Al-Burāq reared once, her mane a shower of moonlight, and with the gentlest of steps, she crossed the threshold between the unseen and the seen.

There, in the city of Mecca, the Prophet Muhammad (peace be upon him) stood in waiting. He had been awoken, not by sound, but by a stirring in the soul. He was calm, though his heart fluttered like a dove sensing the breath of destiny.

And when his eyes beheld Al-Burāq, she lowered her head to him, humbled, not by power, but by her recognition of a pure heart.

"You are the One," she whispered, and knelt so he might mount.

With Jibrīl at his side and the veil of night wrapped around them, the journey began.

In the blink of an eye, they soared from Mecca to Jerusalem, the city of prophets. With each bound of Al-Burāq's hooves, she travelled as far as the eye could see. The winds did not resist her, and the clouds parted before her wings.

They arrived at Al-Aqsa, the farthest mosque, where the Prophet prayed in the company of Abraham, Moses, Jesus, and others who had carried divine light. They stood behind him, recognizing in him the Seal of the Messengers, the final bearer of the trust.

But the journey was not done.

Higher they rose. From the gate of the first heaven, where Adam smiled and welcomed his noble son, to the second, where John and Jesus greeted him, to the third, where Joseph beamed with beauty. Through each heaven, Al-Burāq waited patiently, resting her wings as Jibrīl led the Prophet through gates of light.

In the fourth, he met Idris, the scribe of stars. In the fifth, Aaron opened his arms. In the sixth, stood Moses, who wept not from sorrow, but from awe, knowing the weight his brother would bear. And in the seventh, Abraham, seated by the Lote Tree, welcomed him as kin.

Beyond that, even Jibrīl halted.

"I cannot pass beyond this point," said the angel. "But you may."

And so, alone, the Prophet journeyed further, beyond the Lote Tree of the Utmost Boundary, into a realm where words end and silence becomes meaning. There, in the radiant presence of the Divine, he received that which no soul had received before, namely direct communion, comfort, and command.

He returned with the gift of prayer as ascension for all.

In the blink of a blink, they returned, back to Earth, back to night, and back to the quiet city where people still slept unaware of the vastness that had passed.

Al-Burāq bowed low, and the Prophet dismounted. She looked once more into his eyes, and with a final beat of her wings, vanished into the folds of the unseen, her purpose fulfilled, her waiting complete.

But on the ground where her hooves had touched, flowers grew.

The Demon Horse Race

An Irish Tale

This tale is my version of a brief story in P. W. Joyce's book Old Celtic Romances, published by Longmans, Green And Co., London & New York, in 1920.

Patrick Weston Joyce (1827–1914), known as P. W. Joyce, was a prominent Irish historian, linguist, and folklorist who played a key role in preserving and documenting Ireland's oral traditions, place-names, and cultural heritage during the 19th and early 20th centuries. A member of the Royal Irish Academy and a leading figure in the Gaelic revival, Joyce collected folktales, legends, songs, and proverbs from across Ireland, often drawing from both the Irish and English languages.

Long ago, in the time of sainted voyagers and wandering warriors, a band of men sailed westward beyond the last known headlands of Éire, seeking what lay past the edge of maps and memory. At their head was Maildún, a chieftain born of sorrow and fire, and with him were his companions, brave-hearted souls forged in the winds of exile and bound by blood-oaths and dreams.

They had crossed many leagues of open sea, past islands of flame and birds who sang in forgotten tongues, when, one still morning, they beheld a strange sight rising from the mist: a wide, flat island, green as new rushes, with no cliffs nor peaks to shield it, only a long, even shoreline lapped by softly curling waves.

Now, the custom among the voyagers was to send one man ashore to scout each island they came upon, lest it be cursed or enchanted. And on that day, the lot fell to Germán, a cautious man with eyes like storm clouds.

"It is no happy task," Germán muttered, eyeing the island with suspicion.

But his companion Diurán, fair of speech and bold of step, clapped a hand on his shoulder. "I'll not see you go alone this time, friend," he said. "And the next island that falls to me, you shall walk beside me then. Let us go together and see what gods or ghosts walk this strange land."

And so the two men set out in a small boat and made their way ashore, the others watching from the deck of the curragh with narrowed eyes and silent prayers.

What they found was not what they expected.

The island was vast and oddly still. There were no birds in the sky, nor any breeze in the grass. Yet the land was rich and green, and as they walked, they came upon a great open field, as wide as a king's plain, flat and perfect as though made for sport. And there, marked deep in the turf, were hoof-prints so large that a grown man might lie down inside one and not touch the edges. Each indentation was broad and round, and easily the size of a feasting table or a ship's sail.

Scattered about the field were giant nut-shells, each one as big as a warrior's helm, and here and there were tools of a strange kind, twisted cords of bronze, broken goblets as large as cauldrons, and stones blackened by fire. Yet the field itself was empty.

"No man of flesh left these," said Germán, keeping his voice low.

"They were here," Diurán whispered, "and not long ago."

With fear rising in their bellies, they turned and ran back to the shore, calling out to their comrades. The rest of the crew came quickly, drawn by the urgency in their voices, and when they too saw the giant prints and the monstrous relics scattered like bones, their hearts turned cold. Without delay, they all returned to the boat and began to row hard for open water.

But they had not gone far before the sea itself began to shift. Out of the mist came a thunderous roar, not of storm or wind, but of voices, countless voices, echoing across the waves like the sound of a hundred war-hosts marching together. And then they saw them, a vast multitude of riders, tall as oaks and terrible to behold, moving with inhuman swiftness across the surface of the sea, as though the water were solid ground.

Their skin was as pale as moonlight and their eyes burned like coals. They howled as they rode, not with joy, but with hunger. They were demons, the crew knew, though none dared say it aloud.

The riders did not see the curragh, or if they did, they cared nothing for it. They made straight for the island and gathered in the great field. There, with a crash like a falling sky, they began a horse-race.

The horses they rode were creatures of nightmare, long-legged and sinewed like shadow and smoke, some with manes of fire, others with hooves that sparked when they struck the earth. They flew down the course faster than storm wind, their eyes wild and foam streaking their flanks.

From where Maildún and his men drifted in the sea, they could hear every sound, not faint and distant, but as if they stood among the crowd. They heard the crack of demon whips, the snorts and screams of horses, and the shouts of the monstrous spectators:

"Mind the grey steed, he flies like the hawk!"

"The chestnut! He gains!"

"The white-spotted mare is leaping past them all!"

"Mine is faster than yours, you'll see!"

The seafolk cheered and cursed, and their voices struck the hearts of the men in the boat like iron against bone. It was too much. With fear swelling in their chests, the crew took up the oars and fled, rowing hard, leaving the cursed island behind. And as they vanished into the wide ocean, the sound of the race faded, though for many days after, the dream of the demon horses returned to haunt their sleep.

They spoke no more of the island, save in whispers. For they knew then that they had seen spirits out of the Otherworld, trapped in endless sport, racing for no prize but madness itself.

And so, they called the place ever after: The Isle of the Demon Horse-Race, a place best left unseen, and unspoken, beneath the grey veil of the western sea.

The Horse And The Olive

A Greek Tale

This tale has been adapted from an original by James Baldwin in his book Old Greek Stories, published by the American Book Company, New York, in 1895.

James Baldwin (1841–1925) was an American educator, editor, and prolific author who played a key role in making classical literature, mythology, and folklore accessible to children and young readers in the late 19th and early 20th centuries. A former school superintendent, Baldwin believed strongly in moral instruction through storytelling and wrote or edited more than fifty books that adapted world myths, legends, and historical narratives into simple, engaging prose.

Long ago, before temples crowned the hills and ships crisscrossed the wine-dark seas, there was a steep, stony hill in a wild part of Greece. Upon its rugged peak lived a tribe of people so old and simple that they had yet to build houses or plant crops. They wore skins and slept in caves, and hunted the wild beasts of the forest with sharpened sticks and stones.

Their hilltop offered them protection from prowling animals and wandering warbands, and there was only one narrow path up, guarded day and night by the strongest among them.

One day, while the hunters were scouring the woods for game, they stumbled upon a young man unlike any they had seen. His skin was smooth and golden, his hair long and glinting like sunlight on water, and his garments were fine and strange. He moved like no man they knew, as fluid as a snake and as quick as the wind. The hunters, believing him a creature of magic, a serpent in man's form, were afraid at first. But the youth smiled gently, gestured for food, and when they gave him meat, he bowed his thanks. His gentleness calmed them. They brought him back up the hill, curious to show this wonder to their families.

At first, the people believed they would soon sacrifice him to the spirits they feared. Yet the youth, whose name was Cecrops, was so kind, so joyful, and so wise that even the coldest hearts among them warmed. He played with their children, sang songs of lands beyond the sea, and slowly learned their language. In time, they turned to him for advice. When wolves threatened the hill, he led a defence. When hunger stalked their homes, he taught them new ways to hunt and fish. He showed them how to build huts of wood and thatch, how to live as families, and how to worship the great gods who dwelled in the sky.

And so, Cecrops, who had arrived like a mystery from the sea, was made king. Under his guidance, the hilltop grew from a cluster of caves into a small town with a single gate and sturdy walls. But the town still had no name.

One morning, as Cecrops and his advisors gathered in the market square, planning a future for their people, two figures appeared at the edge of the crowd. No one had seen them enter, for no guard had granted them passage, but they stood tall and regal. One was a man cloaked in green and purple, with a trident in his hand. The other, a woman, carried a spear and a shield, her eyes grey and flashing with divine intelligence.

The man spoke first. "I am Poseidon," he said, his voice like the tide, "lord of the seas."

The woman stepped forward. "And I am Athena," she said, her tone calm but strong, "giver of wisdom and protector of cities."

"We have heard," said Poseidon, "that you seek to make this town great. I offer you my blessing. Name your city for me, and I shall fill your harbour with ships from all the world. You shall grow rich beyond imagining, and master the sea."

"But if you choose me," said Athena, "I shall gift you wisdom and craft. I will teach you how to live well, to think deeply, and to build a city whose spirit shall never die. Let me be your protector, and your fame will outlast all riches."

The people murmured. Some called for wealth, others for wisdom. Seeing the divide, an old man stood and said, "We are offered words and promises of things we do not know. But if these mighty ones give us gifts we can see with our own eyes, we shall know which gift is best."

"Very well," said Poseidon.

He strode to a rocky outcrop and raised his trident high. With a mighty crack, he struck the stone. The earth split, and from the crevice burst a great white creature, muscle-bound, with a flowing mane and hooves of thunder. It was the first horse. The people cried out, some in fear, some in awe.

"This is Horse," said Poseidon. "He will bear you swiftly across the land, draw your wagons and ploughs, and fight beside you in battle."

Then Athena walked to a patch of soft earth where children played. She drove her spear into the ground. At once, music filled the air, and from the soil grew a tree, slender and silver-leaved, its branches heavy with violet-green fruit.

"This is the Olive," she said. "It will nourish you, shade you, heal you, and bring beauty to your home. Its oil will be prized by every nation."

The people fell silent, stunned by both gifts.

Then the same old man spoke again. "Horse is mighty, but we have no carts or ploughs. What use is speed if we do not know where we're going? But Olive offers food, light, healing, and peace. I choose Olive."

And so did the others.

The king turned to Athena. "We choose wisdom," he said. "And from this day forward, our city shall be named Athens."

From that moment, the city flourished. Olive trees spread across the land, and the wisdom of Athena guided Athens through war and peace, art and science, glory and loss. Her temple rose on the highest hill, where it still stands in ruin today. And though Horse galloped north to distant Thessaly, it is said that his kind have never forgotten the hill where they first came into the world.

Thus, by a single choice between wealth and wisdom, a city's soul was born.

The Tale of the Wind Horse

A Tibetan Tale

This is my own version of a traditional legend, written and adapted from various sources and historical notes in my collection of folk and fairy tales.

The legend of the Wind Horse, known as rlung rta in Tibetan and khiimori in Mongolian, is a potent symbol of the human soul and the flow of fortune. Its roots lie deep in Central and East Asian shamanistic traditions, later incorporated into Tibetan Buddhist culture with additional layers of spiritual meaning.

The Wind Horse symbolises the human life force, spiritual resilience, and the uplifting power of well-being, transcending cultural boundaries while evolving through centuries of religion, ritual, and storytelling.

Long before the mountain gods raised the Himalayas like a prayer to the sky, before the yaks carved paths across the clouds, and before the monks carved mantras into stone, the world was young and full of hunger. Men and spirits alike wrestled for breath, for lungta, the sacred wind that moved through all things. Without it, no soul could rise, no fire could burn, no prayer could reach the ears of the gods.

At the centre of this breath, this wind of spirit, there lived a creature not born of flesh or bone but made of will, fire, and sky. Its name was Lungta, the Wind Horse, and its mane was made of cloud-strands, its wings of smoke and thunder. Where it galloped, fortune followed. Where it landed, the air itself turned clear and bright. It carried prayers like seeds on the wind and was said to be the steed of the righteous heart.

But there came a time when the Wind Horse disappeared.

The world noticed first in the turning of prayer flags, those bright cloths strung from peak to peak to carry blessings to the heavens. Once, they danced joyfully in every breeze. Now they hung limp and heavy, their colours fading like forgotten wishes. Crops failed in the high valleys. Merchants found their luck turned sour. And even the lamas in their red robes whispered of a silence in the sky, a stillness in the soul.

In the village of Nyima Drok, perched like a bird's nest on the shoulder of a sacred mountain, a boy named Tempa watched his father's prayer flags fall still. His father, once a great herder and man of strength, now lay coughing in bed, his strength leaking away like a cracked pot leaks water. The monks said it was fate. The traders said it was the cold. But Tempa believed something deeper was broken, something in the breath of the world.

Each night, he would sit beside his father and listen to the stories of the Wind Horse, of how it flew above all things, carrying the lungta of every living being on its back. He heard how it galloped on the wind that flowed between earth and sky, blessing those whose hearts were brave and true.

"But where is it now?" Tempa asked one night.

His father only coughed, then whispered, "Lost. Or stolen."

That night, Tempa dreamed of a sky without stars, a mountain without a summit, and a great winged horse, trapped in a cage of black ice.

Tempa rose before the sun and tied on his father's old sash, woven with the five colours of spirit. He took no pack, no food, only a bundle of prayer flags, old and faded, but still waiting to fly. He walked away from Nyima Drok and began climbing.

Higher and higher he went, past the snow line, where only ghosts and vultures dwell. On the third night, he reached a high pass known only to the oldest of monks, a place where the winds once howled but now fell deathly still. In the silence, he found a single flagpole snapped in half, buried in the snow.

There, Tempa offered the old prayer flags, stringing them from crag to crag. As he did, he sang, not words, but the sound of breath, the sound of memory. And for the first time in years, the air stirred.

From the edge of the cliff, a shadow moved. Then he saw it. The Wind Horse was trapped in a prison of black crystal, its wings pinned by chains of shadow. Around it coiled a great serpent, born of fear and despair, Drakmar, the spirit of suffocating fate.

"Why do you bind it?" Tempa cried.

Drakmar hissed, "The world no longer believes. It no longer sends its prayers, no longer sings its breath. The wind is mine now."

But Tempa was not afraid. He ran toward the cage, his prayer sash whipping like a comet behind him. With each step, he recited the ancient mantra his father taught him: Om mani padme hum. And the wind rose with him. The flags danced. The mountain shook.

The serpent struck, but Tempa threw the flags like knives. The colours became fire, light, and air, and each one cut through the serpent's coils. Red for power. Blue for sky. White for peace. Green for compassion. Yellow for prosperity.

The serpent screamed, unravelling into mist, and the cage shattered. The Wind Horse stood free. It looked at Tempa with eyes of infinite sky, then knelt. Without a word, Tempa climbed on its back, and together they rose into the heavens.

Above the mountains, higher than even the eagles fly, Tempa rode the Wind Horse across the world. Where they passed, prayer flags danced again. Fortune returned. Hearts were lifted. Sick men stood. Crops grew golden.

When he returned to Nyima Drok, his father stood waiting, strong once more. And though Tempa never spoke of what he saw, he often climbed to the highest ridge, where he would tie new prayer flags in the wind, and sometimes, just sometimes, children swore they saw a white winged horse galloping across the clouds, trailing the breath of the world behind it.

The Fire-Bird, The Horse Of Power, And The Princess Vasilissa

A Russian Tale

This is my version of an original story by Arthur Ransome in his book Old Peter's Russian Tales, published by Frederick A. Stokes Co., New York, in 1916.

Arthur Ransome (1884–1967) was a British author, journalist, and folklorist best known for his beloved "Swallows and Amazons" series of children's adventure novels, which celebrated outdoor life, imagination, and independence. Before gaining fame as a novelist, Ransome spent years in Russia as a foreign correspondent during the Russian Revolution, where he developed a deep interest in Russian folklore.

Long ago, in the vast, frost-dusted lands of old Russia, there lived a young man known only as the Archer. Though low in rank, he served in the court of a powerful and temperamental Tsar. But this Archer was not ordinary, for he possessed a horse unlike any the world has seen since. The beast was massive, and coal-black, with hooves like hammered iron and eyes that burned with the light of ancient magic. It was a Horse of Power, a creature born of myths, a companion to heroes.

One day, while riding through a hushed forest, the Archer noticed something strange. Not a single bird was singing. Even the smallest flutter of wings had vanished from the trees. Then he saw a single glowing feather lying across the trail like a dropped flame. It shimmered gold in the sunlight, pulsing with warmth. It was a feather from the Firebird.

As he leaned from the saddle to pick it up, his horse spoke in a low voice like wind across a grave, "Leave it. If you take the feather, you will learn the meaning of fear."

But the Archer thought of his Tsar. He thought of the favour he might earn. And so he ignored the warning, took the feather, and rode back to the palace.

When he presented the feather to the Tsar, the ruler's eyes gleamed with greed. "If you've brought me a feather," he said, "you can bring me the bird. Bring me the Firebird, or lose your head."

The Archer returned to his horse in despair.

"I warned you," said the Horse. "But it is not the end. Ask the Tsar to scatter a hundred sacks of grain in the field by midnight. Then wait."

And so it was done.

At dawn, the Archer hid himself in an old oak overlooking the grain, while his horse grazed in the field below. As the sun crested the edge of the sky, the trees began to shake. Wind howled. Fire crackled in the clouds. And then the

Firebird descended like a comet, its wings throwing golden light over the earth. It landed and began to eat the grain.

The Horse crept close and suddenly stomped hard on one fiery wing, pinning the creature. The Archer sprang from the tree and, with three ropes, bound the magical bird. He lifted it onto his back and carried it to the Tsar.

The Firebird, in all its blazing beauty, now stood at the feet of the Tsar. But the ruler only smiled a cruel smile and said, "Now bring me Princess Vasilissa from the land where the sun rises behind the sea. Only she is fit to be my bride. Fail me, and your head will roll."

The Archer returned to his horse, and he wept.

"Dry your tears," said the Horse of Power. "Ask for a silver tent with golden trim, and enough fine food and wine to fill it. Then ride east with me."

They rode for days, crossing snowy plains and dark woods, until they reached the edge of the world, where dawn rose from the sea like fire. There, in a silver boat with golden oars, rowed Princess Vasilissa, bright-eyed, graceful, and unaware of her fate.

The Archer pitched the silver tent near the shore and set the table with delicacies. When Vasilissa saw the strange shimmering tent, curiosity drew her close. The Archer invited her in. They shared wine, and soon her eyes grew heavy. She drifted into enchanted sleep.

Gently, the Archer lifted her into the saddle and rode hard for the Tsar's court.

When the Princess awoke in the palace, she was bewildered. The sea, her boat, her freedom, all were gone. She saw the Tsar and frowned. But when her eyes fell on the Archer, her heart stirred.

The Tsar declared the wedding would be held at once. But Vasilissa raised her hand. "I will marry no one until I wear the wedding dress hidden beneath the stone in the middle of the sea from which I came."

The Tsar turned to the Archer. "Fetch it, or die."

This time, the journey was harder still, and at the edge of the world, the Archer despaired. But the Horse of Power noticed a great lobster crawling along the shore. He blocked its path and pressed a hoof against its shell.

"Spare me!" cried the lobster.

"Then fetch the dress hidden under the sea-stone," said the Horse.

The lobster called out in a voice that shook the ocean. From all corners of the sea, lobsters swam and scuttled to him. Soon they returned, carrying a golden chest, inside of which was the Princess's wedding dress.

The Archer rode back, and when Vasilissa saw the dress, she smiled, but not at the Tsar. She smiled at the Archer.

Still, the Tsar would not give her up. "Now the wedding!" he bellowed.

But Vasilissa stood tall and said, "Only after the Archer bathes in boiling water will I marry."

The Tsar ordered a great cauldron set on fire. Flames leapt high, water bubbled, and death boiled in the pot. The Archer begged one last moment with his horse.

"Trust me," said the Horse. "Leap into the cauldron."

So the Archer did. He disappeared beneath the frothing surface. All were silent.

Then, he rose. He was no longer a youth, but a vision of manhood, radiant, strong, more handsome than any man the world had known.

The Tsar's eyes widened with envy. If boiling water brought such beauty, he would have it too. He climbed into the pot… And was boiled to death in a breath.

The people buried the Tsar with little mourning, and the Archer was crowned in his place. He married Princess Vasilissa, and ruled with wisdom and kindness.

As for the Horse of Power, he was given a stable of gold and fresh green meadows. But whenever the land grew quiet, the Archer would ride him again across the wide steppes, for the horse was his companion in peace, just as he had been in peril.

And they say that when Russia faces great darkness, the Horse of Power will gallop once more.

The Dun Horse

A Pawnee Tale

This adaptation is taken from a story told by George Bird Grinnell in Pawnee Hero Stories And Folk-Tales, which was originally published by the Forest And Stream Publishing Company, New York, in 1889.

George Bird Grinnell (1849–1938) was an American anthropologist, historian, naturalist, and conservationist best known for his influential work in preserving Native American cultures and protecting natural landscapes. A Yale-educated scholar, he conducted extensive fieldwork among the Plains tribes, especially the Cheyenne and Blackfeet, documenting their oral histories, customs, and beliefs with empathy and depth. Grinnell's books, such as The Fighting Cheyennes and Blackfoot Lodge Tales, remain foundational in American ethnography and folklore.

I

Many years ago, there lived in the Pawnee tribe an old woman and her grandson, a boy about sixteen years old. These people had no relations and were very poor. They were so poor that they were despised by the rest of the tribe. They had nothing of their own, and always, after the village started to move the camp from one place to another, these two would stay behind the rest, to look over the old camp, and pick up anything that the other people had thrown away, as worn out or useless. In this way they would sometimes get pieces of robes, worn out moccasins with holes in them, and bits of meat.

Now, it happened one day, after the tribe had moved away from the camp, that this old woman and her boy were following along the trail behind the rest, when they came to a miserable old worn-out dun horse, which they supposed had been abandoned. He was thin and exhausted, was blind of one eye, had a bad sore back, and one of his forelegs was very much swollen. In fact, he was so worthless that none of the Pawnees had been willing to take the trouble to try to drive him along with them. But when the old woman and her boy came along, the boy said, "Come now, we will take this old horse, for we can make him carry our pack." So the old woman put her pack on the horse, and drove him along, but he limped and could only go very slowly.

II

The tribe moved up on the North Platte, until they came to Court House Rock. The two poor people followed them, and camped with the others. One day while they were here, the young men who had been sent out to look for buffalo, came hurrying into camp and told the chiefs that a large herd of buffalo were near, and that among them was a spotted calf.

The Head Chief of the Pawnees had a very beautiful daughter, and when he heard about the spotted calf, he ordered his old crier to go about through the village, and call out that the man who killed the spotted calf should have his daughter for his wife. For a spotted robe is ti-war´-uks-ti (big medicine).

The buffalo were feeding about four miles from the village, and the chiefs decided that the charge should be made from there. In this way, the man who had the fastest horse would be the most likely to kill the calf. Then all the warriors and the young men picked out their best and fastest horses, and made ready to start. Among those who prepared for the charge was the poor boy on the old dun horse. But when they saw him, all the rich young braves on their fast horses pointed at him, and said, "Oh, see! There is the horse that is going to catch the spotted calf", and they laughed at him, so that the poor boy was ashamed, and rode off to one side of the crowd, where he could not hear their jokes and laughter.

When he had ridden off some little way, the horse stopped, and turned his head round, and spoke to the boy. He said, "Take me down to the creek, and plaster me all over with mud. Cover my head and neck and body and legs."

When the boy heard the horse speak, he was afraid, but he did as he was told. Then the horse said, "Now mount, but do not ride back to the warriors, who laugh at you because you have such a poor horse. Stay right here, until the word is given to charge."

So the boy stayed there.

And presently all the fine horses were drawn up in line and pranced about, and were so eager to go that their riders could hardly hold them in, and at last the old crier gave the word, "Loo-ah, Go!"

Then the Pawnees all leaned forward on their horses and yelled, and away they went. Suddenly, away off to the right, was seen the old dun horse. He did not seem to run. He seemed to sail along like a bird. He passed all the fastest horses, and in a moment he was among the buffalo. First he picked out the spotted calf, and charging up alongside of it, straight flew the arrow. The calf fell. The boy drew another arrow, and killed a fat cow that was running by. Then he dismounted and began to skin the calf before any of the other warriors had come up. But when the rider got off the old dun horse, how changed he was! He pranced about and would hardly stand still near the dead buffalo. His back was all right again, his legs were well and fine, and both his eyes were clear and bright.

The boy skinned the calf and the cow that he had killed, and then he packed all the meat on the horse, and put the spotted robe on top of the load, and started back to the camp on foot, leading the dun horse. But even with this heavy load the horse pranced all the time, and was scared at everything he saw. On the way to camp, one of the rich young chiefs of the tribe rode up by the boy, and offered him twelve good horses for the spotted robe, so that he could marry the Head Chief's beautiful daughter, but the boy laughed at him and would not sell the robe.

Now, while the boy walked to the camp leading the dun horse, most of the warriors rode back, and one of those that came first to the village, went to the old woman, and said to her, "Your grandson has killed the spotted calf."

And the old woman said, "Why do you come to tell me this? You ought to be ashamed to make fun of my boy, because he is poor."

The warrior said, "What I have told you is true," and then he rode away. After a little while another brave rode up to the old woman, and said to her, "Your grandson has killed the spotted calf."

Then the old woman began to cry, she felt so badly because everyone made fun of her boy, because he was poor.

Pretty soon the boy came along, leading the horse up to the lodge where he and his grandmother lived. It was a little lodge, just big enough for two, and was made of old pieces of skin that the old woman had picked up, and was tied together with strings of rawhide and sinew. It was the meanest and worst lodge in the village. When the old woman saw her boy leading the dun horse with the load of meat and the robes on it, she was very much surprised.

The boy said to her, "Here, I have brought you plenty of meat to eat, and here is a robe, that you may have for yourself. Take the meat off the horse."

Then the old woman laughed, for her heart was glad. But when she went to take the meat from the horse's back, he snorted and jumped about, and acted like a wild horse. The old woman looked at him in wonder, and could hardly believe that it was the same horse. So the boy had to take off the meat, for the horse would not let the old woman come near him.

III

That night the horse spoke again to the boy and said, "Wa-ti-hes Chah´-ra-rat wa-ta. Tomorrow the Sioux are coming with a large war party. They will attack the village, and you will have a great battle. Now, when the Sioux are drawn up in line of battle, and are all ready to fight, you jump on to me, and ride as hard as you can, right into the middle of the Sioux, and up to their Head Chief, their greatest warrior and kill him, and then ride back. Do this four times, and count coup (gain prestige) on four of the bravest Sioux, and kill them, but don't go again. If you go the fifth time, may be you will be killed, or else you will lose me. La-ku´-ta-chix, remember." So the boy promised.

The next day it happened as the horse had said, and the Sioux came down and formed a line of battle. Then the boy took his bow and arrows, and jumped on the dun horse, and charged into the midst of them. And when the Sioux saw that he was going to strike their Head Chief, they all shot their arrows at him, and the arrows flew so thickly across each other that the sky became dark, but none of them hit the boy. And he counted coup on the Chief, and killed him, and then rode back. After that he charged again among the Sioux, where they were gathered thickest, and counted coup on their bravest warrior, and killed him. And then twice more, until he had gone four times as the horse had told him.

But the Sioux and the Pawnees kept on fighting, and the boy stood around and watched the battle. And at last he said to himself, "I have been four times and have killed four Sioux, and I am all right, I am not hurt anywhere. Why may I not go again?" So he jumped on the dun horse, and charged again.

But when he got among the Sioux, one Sioux warrior drew an arrow and shot. The arrow struck the dun horse behind the forelegs and pierced him through. And the horse fell down dead. But the boy jumped off, and fought his way through the Sioux, and ran away as fast as he could to the Pawnees. Now, as soon as the horse was killed, the Sioux said to each other, "This horse was like a man. He was brave. He was not like a horse." And they took their knives and hatchets, and hacked the dun horse and gashed his flesh, and cut him into small pieces.

The Pawnees and Sioux fought all day long, but toward night the Sioux broke and fled.

IV

The boy felt very badly that he had lost his horse, and, after the fight was over, he went out from the village to where the battle had taken place, to mourn for his horse. He went to the spot where the horse lay, and gathered up all the pieces of flesh, which the Sioux had cut off, and the legs and the hoofs, and put them all together in a pile. Then he went off to the top of a hill nearby, and sat down and drew his robe over his head, and began to mourn for his horse.

As he sat there, he heard a great windstorm coming up, and it passed over him with a loud rushing sound, and after the wind came a rain. The boy looked down from where he sat to the pile of flesh and bones, which was all that was left of his horse, and he could just see it through the rain. And the rain passed by, and his heart was very heavy, and he kept on mourning.

And pretty soon, came another rushing wind, and after it a rain, and as he looked through the driving rain toward the spot where the pieces lay, he thought that they seemed to come together and take shape, and that the pile looked like a horse lying down, but he could not see well for the thick rain.

After this, came a third storm like the others, and now when he looked toward the horse he thought he saw its tail move from side to side two or three times, and that it lifted its head from the ground. The boy was afraid, and wanted to run away, but he stayed where he was.

And as he waited, there came another storm. And while the rain fell, looking through the rain, the boy saw the horse raise himself up on his forelegs and look about. Then the dun horse stood up.

V

The boy left the place where he had been sitting on the hilltop, and went down to the horse. When the boy had come near to him, the horse spoke and said, "You have seen how it has been this day, and from this you may know how it will be after this. But Ti-ra´-wa has been good, and has let me come back to you. After this, do what I tell you. Never more, nor any less." Then the horse said, "Now lead me off, far away from the camp, behind that big hill, and leave me there tonight, and in the morning come for me." The boy did as he was told.

And when he went for the horse in the morning, he found with him a beautiful white gelding, much more handsome than any horse in the tribe. That night the dun horse told the boy to take him again to the place behind the big hill, and to come for him the next morning, and when the boy went for him again, he found with him a beautiful black gelding. And so for ten nights, he left the horse among the hills, and each morning he found a different coloured horse, a bay, a roan, a grey, a blue, a spotted horse, and all of them finer than any horses that the Pawnees had ever had in their tribe before.

Now the boy was rich, and he married the beautiful daughter of the Head Chief, and when he became older, he was made Head Chief himself. He had many children by his beautiful wife, and one day when his oldest boy died, he wrapped him in the spotted calf robe and buried him in it. He always took good care of his old grandmother, and kept her in his own lodge until she died. The dun horse was never ridden except at feasts, and when they were going to have a doctors' dance, but he was always led about with the Chief, wherever he went. The horse lived in the village for many years, until he became very old. And at last he died.

The Salt-Breath of the Nuckelavee

An Orkney Tale

This is my own version of a traditional legend, written and adapted from various sources and historical notes in my collection of folk and fairy tales. The Salt-Breath of the Nuckelavee originates in Orcadian folklore, the traditions of the Orkney Islands, off the northern coast of Scotland.

The Nuckelavee is a terrifying sea-demon, often described as a skinless horse-like monster with a human rider fused to its back. The only force said to restrain it was the spirit of the Mither o' the Sea (the Mother of the Sea), who kept it bound during summer months. In winter, however, the creature roamed freely, striking terror in the people.

The tale was recorded most famously in the 19th century by Walter Traill Dennison, an Orcadian folklorist, who preserved local accounts of the Nuckelavee's monstrous form and deadly breath in his collection of Orkney traditions.

The villagers of Aith sat with their backs to the sea. It had been that way for generations, homes turned inland, windows shuttered tight against the sound of the surf. Not for fear of storm, nor pirate, nor salt wind, but for something older, something the islanders spoke of only when drunk or dying.

They called it Him. The Nuckelavee.

He had no skin, they said. No eyes, and yet he saw. A great, glistening horse's body fused with the torso of a man, its mouth stitched into a permanent scream. Muscles red and slick as butcher's meat. His breath was said to rot crops in the ground, sour milk in the udder, and blister a child's lungs before its first word.

Old Mother Cairn claimed to have seen Him once, as a girl. She had spoken of His coming like the arrival of sickness in spring, the way animals cried and the wind changed taste.

"I heard the sea laugh," she said once, rocking slowly before her peat fire. "It sounded like a man drowning slow."

None believed her.

That was until the cattle began to die, eyes weeping yellow and legs trembling like thawing ice, until the black scab spread across the barley, until the smokehouse reeked of sulphur, though no peat was lit. That was the year the sea came for the island again.

Duncan Gray was the only one who still walked the causeway by moonlight. He was the lighthouse keeper's son, and though the light had long gone dark, extinguished when the government declared the rock unmanned, Duncan returned to it as though called. He said nothing to the others, only nodded and stepped out across the narrow spit of stone that vanished at high tide, leading into the sea's throat.

Some said grief had ruined him. His mother had been taken by fever, and his sister washed out in a storm. Others said he simply didn't care if he lived or died. But Duncan was not careless. He walked the causeway with purpose, lantern swinging low, salt thick in his throat. He did not fear the Nuckelavee. He was looking for him.

It was the third night of the new moon when Duncan first saw the beast. He stood at the end of the causeway, just past the tide's reach. No boat. No birds. Just fog and foam.

Then came the sound, not a gallop but a squelch, a dragging of meat across stone. A figure rose from the mist. Duncan saw the form of a horse without skin, each tendon exposed, its hooves black and steaming. Atop it, fused like a tumour, there was a man with elongated arms, no lips, his mouth a raw hole of gnashing teeth.

"You called me," the thing rasped, breath like sour milk. "Why?"

Duncan swallowed, but his voice held firm. "You took my sister."

The Nuckelavee tilted its head. "She was mine by debt. You gave her when you cried out that night in grief. You said: Take anything, just don't let her die."

"I was a boy."

"Aye," the creature smiled with no lips, "and promises made by boys are all the sweeter."

Duncan stepped forward, closer than any man should. "Take me instead."

A wheeze, like the sea exhaling, escaped the Nuckelavee.

"I do not trade."

But then his head twisted, his eyes like pits. "Unless…"

*

The villagers awoke to screaming. The fields smoked. The sea stank of iron. Every well ran red. And Duncan did not return from his nightly vigil.

But the plague stopped. The livestock healed. The barley came back green, and even Old Mother Cairn lived long enough to blink in shock. That was when they rebuilt the lighthouse and painted it white.

But the islanders still kept their windows shuttered, because sometimes, on a new moon, if the wind was right, you could hear hooves on the stone causeway, wet and slow.

And if you listened longer, you'd hear something else, a voice, not the Nuckelavee's, but a man's voice, screaming. It sounded like an endless bargaining rather than a voice in pain It sounded like a promise remade and a debt never paid.

*

Many years later a child found a lantern on the beach. It was old, and crusted with salt, but the glass was clean, the flame inside still warm. Inside the glass, carved faintly, was a name: Duncan Gray.

The islanders burned that lantern without a word being said, because they knew the truth. The Nuckelavee is not a monster of rage, nor is he a demon of impulse. He is patient. He waits for the taste of fear, for the sound of desperation in a man's voice. He does not come from the sea. He is the sea.

Unforgiving. Skinless. Eternal. And he never forgets what he is owed.

The Story Of The Horse, The Lion, And The Wolf

A Romanian Tale

This adaptation is taken from a story told by Moses Gaster in Rumanian Bird and Beast Stories, which was originally published by Sidgwick And Jackson, London, in 1915.

Moses Gaster (1856–1939) was a Romanian-born British scholar, rabbi, and folklorist known for his significant contributions to the study of Jewish folklore, literature, and linguistics. He was especially influential in collecting and publishing Romanian and Sephardic Jewish folk tales, preserving many oral traditions that might otherwise have been lost. Gaster served as Chief Rabbi of the Sephardic Jewish community in Britain and was a leading authority on Samaritan texts and Jewish mysticism.

There once lived a Sultan who had a charger. It had served him most faithfully for a good number of years, carrying him in many battles and on numerous other occasions.

At last the horse grew old and was no longer fit to serve him as before. The Sultan, remembering its faithful services, decided to free it from every manner of work, and in token of recognition of its faithfulness he set it free to roam about and to feed wherever it liked.

In order that it should not be molested, he ordered that a special coat should be made for it of red cloth adorned with many coloured stripes and patches. He also had it shod with steel shoes, which last for a very long time.

So, covered with the king's cloth, the horse went about from field to field eating whatever and whenever it pleased. Being now at ease, the horse got fat again and strong, and when it walked on the road, it struck with its feet against the stones and pebbles, and made the sparks fly from them.

In a nearby forest there lived a lion. One day, coming out to the edge of the wood, he saw the horse in the distance, and as he had never yet seen such a peculiar animal, he got frightened and started running back into the thickest part of the forest.

There he met a wolf, who, seeing the lion run, asked him why he was running.

"If your life is dear to you," he replied, "do not stop here talking, for that terrible beast which I have seen yonder in the field is sure to overtake us, and then good-bye to us."

"What beast?" asked the wolf. "I know no beast that could frighten a lion."

"Well, then, thank God that you have never come across it."

"How does it look?"

"It is a huge beast with a head so big as I have never seen a head before, and a mouth so large that it could devour us in one bite. As to its skin, I have never yet seen any like it, all red with stripes and patches of every colour. It stands on huge feet, and whenever it walks it scatters fire right and left."

"That may all be as you describe it," said the wolf, "but still it might also be otherwise. I should like to see it myself, and I might perhaps know what it is."

"Very well then, let us go higher up the hill, where we can look down on the field."

"I would rather see it from here, if possible, near at hand."

"As you please. I will squat down on my hind-legs and lift you up with my fore-legs, so that you can see some distance from here."

The lion did as he said, and taking the wolf in his fore-paws he lifted him up. But whilst doing so he pressed the wolf so hard that he nearly lost his breath, and his eyes began starting out of his head. When the lion saw it, he said, "You cur, you talk bravely and laugh at me who has been close to that terrible beast, and you, who are so far away and scarcely able to get a glimpse of it, you are already losing your breath, and your eyes are starting out of your head."

With these words he threw the wolf down, and away he ran as fast as his legs would carry him.

The Sun-Horse

An Indigenous South African Tale

This is my version of a very short piece told by James A. Honey in South-African Folk-Tales, which was originally published by The Baker & Taylor Company, New York, in 1910.

James A. Honey was an American folklorist and compiler best known for his work collecting and preserving legends and folklore during the late 19th century. His most notable contribution is the book Hawaiian Folk Tales: A Collection of Native Legends, published in 1907, which gathers traditional myths, hero tales, and religious stories from Hawaii.

Long, long ago, when the land was still young and wild, before the Sun climbed into the sky forever, it walked among the living things on the earth. The rivers had no names, the mountains were sleeping, and all creatures, small and great, knew that the world was being shaped by mighty hands.

One day, the Sun walked across the grasslands of what would one day be known as the Karoo. It was not yet blazing in the heavens, but was a golden being who shimmered like fire and cast long shadows even in the noonday light. The Sun was on a journey to rise into the sky and take its rightful place above the earth, but first, it needed a creature strong and noble to carry it to the sacred mountain where it would rise for the last time.

The Sun looked out over the plains and saw the Horse, proud and swift, with a mane like rippling clouds and legs that thundered like distant drums when it galloped. The Sun called to Horse and said, "Come, you who are born to run with the wind. Carry me to the sacred mountain, and I shall bless you with strength unending and make your name great among all beasts."

The Horse, proud as it was, stepped forward and bowed its noble head. "I will carry you, Bright One," said Horse, and knelt to let the Sun mount its back.

But the moment the Sun sat upon the Horse, the beast shuddered. The Sun's heat, even in its human form, was unbearable. The fire of it sank into the Horse's bones. Its legs buckled, and its breath grew short. The Horse stumbled and cried out, "Forgive me, great Sun, I cannot bear your weight!"

The Sun looked down at the trembling Horse with eyes like molten gold. "You were made proud, but not strong. You were swift, but not enduring. You cannot carry the fire of the heavens."

And with that, the Sun stepped down and turned its gaze to the Ox. The Ox stood nearby, watching with quiet eyes. Its body was broad, its pace slow, but its heart was steady. The

Sun called to it, "Come, one who toils without complaint. Bear me to the sacred mountain."

The Ox lowered its head and bore the Sun across the burning plains. Its hooves cracked dry earth, and its back did not bend beneath the golden weight. The Ox climbed the mountain, and when it reached the peak, the Sun rose from its back and leapt into the sky, never to walk the earth again.

But the Horse was left behind, weary and ashamed.

Before the Sun vanished into the heavens, it turned once more to the Horse and said, "Because you could not carry me, your life shall be cursed with hunger and restlessness."

And the Sun's voice thundered across the land:

"From this day onward, your time shall be counted.

You shall not live forever as once it was meant.

You shall graze from dawn until dusk,

Yet your heart shall never be full.

The hunger in your belly shall not quiet your longing.

You shall fear the fire I carry, and shiver at the shadows it casts.

This is my judgment, and it shall follow your kind forever."

And so it is. To this day, the Horse roams the plains and mountains, eating always, but never satisfied. Its eyes hold a distant sadness, as if it remembers the time it might have carried the Sun itself. It fears fire, though it has never known why. And when the day ends, and the last golden light slips from the earth, it pauses, ears twitching, as if listening for the Sun's judgment whispered once more across the wind.

Thus ends the tale of the Horse who refused the Sun.

The Backwards Riders of Storr Rock

A Folk Tale Of Skye

This is my interpretation based on a factual note by John Gregorson Campbell in Superstitions of the Highlands and Islands of Scotland, which was originally published by James Maclehose and Sons, Glasgow, in 1900.

John Gregorson Campbell (1834–1891) was a Scottish folklorist and parish minister known for his meticulous collection and preservation of Highland folklore and mythology. Despite his role as a clergyman, he had a deep respect for traditional beliefs and made it his mission to document the oral tales of the Gaelic-speaking communities of the Hebrides and the Scottish Highlands before they disappeared.

Long ago, when the wind still howled the old tongue through the glens and the mountains listened like sleeping giants, there was a place called Ruig at the foot of the Storr Rock, in the north of Skye. It was a hard land, worked by harder people, sixteen small farming families, living close to the stone, to the sea, and to one another. They kept sheep and cattle, and of course, horses, strong island beasts bred to haul stone, plough fields, and carry men through mists so thick they could bury a memory.

Now, Ruig was a quiet enough place most days, though the cliffs that edged the farm fell sheer into the sea below. The old people said that the ground near Storr Rock was thin in the way cloth gets thin with too much wear. And where the land is thin, they said, other things may come through.

The young people laughed at such talk, and even the old ones mostly kept their fears tucked behind their teeth. But everyone, young or old, bold or pious, stayed in on Hallowmas Night.

That year, the wind turned sharp before Samhain. The sea had a silvery skin and the sheep were bleating with no reason under the stars. The people of Ruig, all sixteen families, gathered in their crofts, shuttered and tight, with fire on the hearth and iron in the doorframes. Not a soul dared roam, save for a boy named Padruig, the blacksmith's son, whose curiosity was larger than his fear.

Padruig was young, but not stupid. He kept a hag-stone on a cord around his neck and a bit of rowan twig in his coat pocket. Just before midnight, he crept out of his family's byre and climbed the ridge to look down on the fields where the horses were kept.

What he saw made his heart freeze in his chest.

All across the pasture, the horses had gathered, mares and stallions, old geldings and skittish colts. They stood as still as cairn stones under the moon, steaming and strangely quiet. Then, from the shadows, the Fair Folk came.

Padruig had never seen them before, not directly, but he knew what they were, for no human moved like that, like drifting smoke with feet. They wore no shoes, and their clothes shimmered like water. Their eyes caught the moon and held it. And strangest of all, they mounted the horses not in the way of men. not forward, but backwards, their faces turned to the tails, their spines straight and stiff.

The horses reared and bucked as if some madness, the cuthach dearg, the red fury, had gripped them. They screamed and took off in a thunder of hooves toward the cliffs.

Padruig gasped aloud. He was sure they would plunge over the edge, beast and rider both, into the black sea below.

He ran back to the village, yelling of what he'd seen, but when the people of Ruig came with lanterns and torches at dawn, they found the horses grazing calmly in the lower fields, with not a hair out of place. There was no evidence of cuts, nor sweat, nor broken hoof. All was peaceful.

And yet… not all was as it had been.

From that day, the horses were never the same. They shied at shadows they once ignored. They refused to work on Samhain's eve. One or two, once docile, now bit and kicked as though remembering something that clawed at their psyche. Among the foals born the next spring, one had eyes like silver coins and a stripe down its back that no man could brush clean.

Padruig never again dared spy on the hollow nights.

The old folk still say that the Fairies come riding only where the veil thins, where cliff meets mist, where silence grows deep, and where the earth remembers older things than men.

And every Hallowmas since, at Ruig beneath the Storr, the farmers keep their horses locked and their windows closed. But if the wind is right, and the night clear, sometimes you can hear hooves on stone racing toward the sea, and the high, keening laughter of those who ride with their faces to the tail.

And may you never see them,

Nor hear their call,

But if you do, don't answer,

And don't watch them fall.

Theo And His Horses; Jane, Betsy, And Blanche

A French Tale

This story has been adapted from a tale told by Andrew Lang in The Animal Story Book, which was originally published by Longmans, Green And Co., London & New York, in 1896. This story was originally taken from Ménagerie Intime.

Andrew Lang (1844–1912) was a Scottish poet, novelist, literary critic, and folklorist best known for his influential work in collecting and popularizing folk and fairy tales from around the world. While Lang often served as editor and commentator, much of the translation and collection work was done by his wife, Leonora Blanche Alleyne. Lang's writings helped revive interest in folklore and mythology during the Victorian era and laid a foundation for modern comparative folklore studies.

After Théophile grew to be a man, he wrote a great many books, which are all delightful to read, and everybody bought them, and Théophile got rich and thought he might give himself a little carriage with two horses to draw it.

First he fell in love with two dear little Shetland ponies who were so shaggy and hairy that they seemed all mane and tail, and whose eyes looked so affectionately at him, that he felt as if he should like to bring them into the drawing-room instead of sending them to the stable. They were charming little creatures, not a bit shy, and they would come and poke their noses into Théophile's pockets in search for sugar, which was always there. Indeed their only fault was, that they were so very, very small, and that, after all, was not their fault. Still, they looked more suited to an English child of eight years old, or to Tom Thumb, than to a French gentleman of forty, not so thin as he once was, and as they all passed through the streets, everybody laughed, and drew pictures of them, and declared that Théophile could easily have carried a pony on each arm, and the carriage on his back.

Now Théophile did not mind being laughed at, but still he did not always want to be stared at all through the streets, whenever he went out. So he sold his ponies and began to look out for something nearer his own size. After a short search he found two of a dapple grey colour, stout and strong, and as like each other as two peas, and he called them Jane and Betsy. But although, to look at, no one could ever tell one from the other, their characters were totally different, as Jane was very bold and spirited, and Betsy was terribly lazy. While Jane did all the pulling, Betsy was quite contented just to run by her side, without troubling herself in the least, and, as was only natural, Jane did not think this at all fair, and took a great dislike to Betsy, which Betsy heartily returned. At last matters became so bad that, in their efforts to get at each other, they half kicked the stable to pieces, and would even rear themselves upon their hind legs in order to bite each other's faces.

Théophile did all he could to make them friends, but nothing was of any use, and at last he was forced to sell Betsy. The horse he found to replace her was a shade lighter in colour, and therefore not quite so good a match, but luckily Jane took to her at once, and lost no time in doing the honours of the stable. Every day the affection between the two became greater: Jane would lay her head on Blanche's shoulder, for she had been called Blanche because of her fair skin, and when they were turned out into the stable-yard, after being rubbed down, they played together like two kittens. If one was taken out alone, the other became sad and gloomy, till the well-known tread of its friend's hoofs was heard from afar, when it would give a joyful neigh, which was instantly answered.

Never once was it necessary for the coachman to complain of any difficulty in harnessing them. They walked themselves into their proper places, and behaved in all ways as if they were well brought up, and ready to be friendly with everybody. They had all kinds of pretty little ways, and if they thought there was a chance of getting bread or sugar or melon rind, which they both loved, they would make themselves as caressing as a dog.

Nobody who has lived much with animals can doubt that they talk together in a language that man is too stupid to understand, or, if anyone had doubted it, they would soon have been convinced of the fact by the conduct of Jane and Blanche when in harness. When Jane first made Blanche's acquaintance, she was afraid of nothing, but after they had been together a few months, her character gradually changed, and she had sudden panics and nervous fits, which puzzled her master greatly. The reason of this was that Blanche, who was very timid and easily frightened, passed most of the night in telling Jane ghost stories, till poor Jane learnt to tremble at every sound.

Often, when they were driving in the lonely alleys of the Bois de Boulogne after dark, Blanche would come to a dead stop or shy to one side as if a ghost, which no one else could see, stood before her. She breathed loudly, trembled all over with fear, and broke out into a cold perspiration. No efforts of Jane, strong though she was, could drag her along. The only way to move her was for the coachman to dismount, and to lead her, with his hand over her eyes for a few steps, till the vision seemed to have melted into air. In the end, these terrors affected Jane just as if Blanche, on reaching the stable, had told her some terrible story of what she had seen, and even her master had been known to confess that when, driving by moonlight down some dark road, where the trees cast strange shadows, Blanche would suddenly come to a dead halt and begin to tremble, he did not half like it himself.

With this one drawback, never were animals so charming to drive. If Théophile held the reins, it was really only for the look of the thing, and not in the least because it was necessary. The smallest click of the tongue was enough to direct them, to quicken them, to make them go to the right or to the left, or even to stop them. They were so clever that in a very short time they had learned all their master's habits, and knew his daily haunts as well as he did himself. They would go of their own accord to the newspaper office, to the printing office, to the publisher's, to the Bois de Boulogne, to certain houses where he dined on certain days in the week, so very punctually that it was quite provoking; and if it ever happened that Théophile spent longer than usual at any particular place, they never failed to call his attention by loud neighs, or by pawing the ground, sounds of which he quite well knew the meaning.

But alas, the time came when a Revolution broke out in Paris. People had no time to buy books or to read them, for they were far too busy in building barricades across the streets, or in tearing up the paving stones to throw at each other. The newspaper in which Théophile wrote, and which paid him enough money to keep his horses, did not appear any more, and sad though he was at parting, the poor man thought he was lucky to find someone to buy horses, carriage, and harness, for a fourth part of their worth. Tears stood in his eyes as they were led away to their new stable, but he never forgot them, and they never forgot him. Sometimes, as he sat writing at his table, he would hear from afar a light quick step, and then a sudden stop under the windows.

And their old master would look up and sigh and say to himself, "Poor Jane, poor Blanche, I hope they are happy."

Bayard, The Magical Horse

A French Tale

This is my own version of a traditional legend, written and adapted from various sources and historical notes in my collection of folk and fairy tales. This is a tale of the age of Charlemagne, originating from medieval French and wider European chivalric traditions.

Bayard became a symbol of loyalty and resistance against tyranny, as he served the four brothers in their rebellion. In folklore of the Ardennes and Wallonia, Bayard is said still to haunt rivers and woods, a proud, untamed spirit of freedom and defiance.

In an age when the sun never rose without the clash of swords and the courts of kings echoed with the oaths of men bound by iron and blood, there lived a horse unlike any other. His name was Bayard, a great bay stallion, foaled not by any earthly mare but conjured from sorcery and song, given life by the wizard Maugis, nephew to the noble house of Montauban.

Bayard had eyes like storm clouds and a coat like burnished bronze. He was as swift as the wind that dances over wheat fields, as wise as any man, and strong enough to bear not one, but four armoured knights upon his back without tiring. Some said he could leap the breadth of a river in a single bound. Others whispered that he understood the words of men, and judged them in silence.

But Bayard chose only one knight as his master, and that was Renaud de Montauban, the fiercest and most loyal of the four sons of Duke Aymon. Renaud, tall and proud, bore a sword forged from Damascus steel, although his heart was wounded by the bitter weight of honour.

Renaud and his three brothers, Richard, Alard, and Guichard, served under Charlemagne, Emperor of the Franks, whose beard was as white as snow and whose fury burned like a smith's forge. One day, in a moment of hot temper and pride, Renaud killed the emperor's nephew in a quarrel during a game of chess. The blow was swift and fatal from a golden chess board used as a weapon, irony forged into tragedy.

The court fell silent. Vengeance was demanded. Charlemagne, bound by law and blood, called for Renaud's execution.

The four brothers fled, and with them fled Bayard leaping over the River Meuse in a single bound, carrying them like leaves in a gale. Wherever they went, Bayard was their shadow and their salvation. His hooves crushed the soil of Burgundy, the forests of Ardennes, and the peaks of Auvergne. Armies were outpaced and traps were sprung. Siege and snow could not stop them.

Bayard had been a gift from Maugis, Renaud's cousin and a sorcerer raised by faeries in the deep woods. Maugis had stolen the horse from Hell itself, or so the minstrels sang, and tamed the beast with spells whispered under moonlight.

Bayard knew battle as well as any knight. He danced between arrows, crushed foes beneath iron hooves, and shielded Renaud with his own great body. At night, he would graze quietly, his breath steaming in the cold, his ears pricking to distant threats. He needed no reins. Renaud had but to think, and Bayard obeyed.

Years passed in war and wandering. Eventually, Charlemagne grew weary and the people began to whisper . Not all praised the emperor for hunting his own blood, and so he offered peace. If Renaud would surrender Bayard, he might earn forgiveness and return to court.

It was no light thing. Bayard had become more than a mount, he was Renaud's soul made flesh, the last pure thing left in a life torn by feud. But Renaud was tired too. His brothers were aging, their children growing and their hunger for home gnawed at the brothers louder than glory. With a heavy heart, he agreed.

Charlemagne demanded Bayard be drowned in the River Meuse, to ensure the magical beast would never serve another rebel. They led the great horse to the water, chaining him with stones and iron. Renaud turned his face away as the executioners struck him.

But Bayard would not die.

He reared, broke the chains with a cry like thunder, and vanished into the forest and into legend. Some say he waits still, deep in the green, by a hidden spring where he drinks under the stars, immortal and alone. Others say Maugis called him back to the realm of the fae, where time forgets.

*

To complete the tale, Renaud lived the rest of his days as a penitent. He became a builder of churches, his sword left to rust in a forgotten hall. When he died, betrayed once more by men jealous of his fame, the people mourned not just a warrior, but a man who had once ridden with the wind.

As for Bayard, his hoofprints remain etched in stone near the Meuse. Farmers find them in the fields after the rain. Children swear they hear him gallop past in stormy nights, bearing unseen riders across the darkened hills, because some magic never dies, and some horses are more than mortal.

Alastair na Bèisde and the Loch of the Woman

A Folk Tale Of Raasay (Scotland)

This is my interpretation based on a factual note by John Gregorson Campbell in Superstitions of the Highlands and Islands of Scotland, which was originally published by James Maclehose and Sons, Glasgow, in 1900.

His most notable works include The Fairy-Faith in Celtic Countries and Superstitions of the Highlands and Islands of Scotland, where he recorded stories of fairies, second sight, water horses, and other supernatural beings. Campbell's writing style was careful and faithful to the original storytellers' voices, preserving the rhythms and imagery of the oral tradition.

Long ago, on the rugged Isle of Raasay, nestled between the cliffs and heathered moors, there lay a dark little loch beneath the looming shadow of Dùn Càn, the highest peak in the land. This loch was known to all the crofters and clansfolk as Loch na Mna, the Woman's Loch, and not without cause, for it was whispered at firesides and over winter drams that a creature, an Each Uisge, a Water-horse of dreadful cunning, had taken up its haunt there. Worse still, it had once lured a woman from her home and dragged her beneath the surface, never to be seen again.

The tale of her loss lingered, like mist on the moors. Some said the water-horse had taken her in the shape of a fine black stallion, standing by the loch with a mane that shimmered like seaweed in moonlight. Others claimed it sang like a man and stepped lightly like a lover until its back was mounted. and then, no rider ever returned. All agreed, though, that the creature was unnatural, a shapeshifter of old magic, and that Loch na Mna had grown dark since the woman's vanishing, its waters always rippling though no wind blew across them.

In a croft not far from the cursed loch lived a man known only as An Gobha Mòr, the Big Smith. His name was Alastair, a man of towering height and arms like iron bands, with hair the colour of peat ash and eyes as keen as flint. He worked a forge that glowed day and night, shaping ploughs, blades, and bridles, and it was said no tool of his had ever failed. But Alastair was a quiet man, and folk didn't often guess the sorrow he carried.

You see, the woman who had vanished was his sister.

They had been bairns together, reared by the same fire, and he had sworn on the hilt of their father's dirk that he'd find the beast who'd taken her. It had taken years of listening to the wind and the waters, years of waiting for the right day, the right wind, the right plan. But one morning, as the rowan trees blossomed and the eagles circled high over Dùn Càn, Alastair stood from his anvil and said to the wind, "Today."

He took no steel blade. Instead, he built himself a hut of stone and peat beside Loch na Mna, low and clever, with a narrow drain-like opening no wider than a beast's body. From that slit the wind could carry scent and smoke down across the still water. Inside, he placed a hearth, a rack of fire-hot irons, and the body of a wether sheep he'd slaughtered and seasoned with sweet herbs from the hill.

All day the wind blew westward, just as he'd hoped. The smell of roasting meat drifted in threads over the loch's surface like spirit-fingers. And from somewhere below the dark water, there came a stirring.

Alastair waited. The forge-irons in the fire glowed as white as starlight. His arms, bare to the shoulder, were smeared with soot and salt. His breath made no sound. Then, as the sun dipped behind the crags, the Water-horse came.

It did not come as a stallion, nor as a man. It slid from the loch like a shadow peeled from the water, its shape lurching and shifting, first hooved, then limbed, then legless again. Its hide was as grey as old turf, slick with slime and dripping with weeds, and its eyes glowed like coals deep under the peat. It snorted once, inhaling the air like a hound on scent, and moved toward the hut.

It crawled inside, squeezing through the syver opening, drawn to the smell of meat like a starving hound. And as its bulk passed over the threshold, Alastair rose. He seized the tongs. With both hands, he gripped the red-hot irons and drove them into the beast's flank. The Water-horse screamed, not in a beast's voice, but in something other. The hut shook. The loch outside boiled. But Alastair pressed on, jabbing iron into jelly-flesh, and holding the creature down with all the strength in his body.

At last, with a final shriek that shattered the air like a dirk through glass, the Water-horse crumpled. Its flesh melted into a mass of grey turf and oily jelly, leaving no bone, no blood, no hide, only a reek of brine and peat rot.

Alastair staggered back, singed and battered, and stared at the remains. There was nothing left to bury. Nothing left to burn. But he knew, in his heart, that the thing which had haunted Loch na Mna, the thing that had stolen his sister, was gone.

From that day forward, the loch grew still. The mists lifted. Birds returned to sing in the reeds, and no horse, water-born or otherwise, was ever seen by Dùn Càn again.

And Alastair, though he never married nor boasted of his deed, came to be called Alastair na Bèisde, Alexander of the Monster. The name stayed with him until his death, and they say even now, when the wind is right and the loch is still, you can smell roast mutton on the air, and the faint ring of hammer on iron, echoing up from the peat.

The War Horse Of Alexander

A Greek Tale

This story has been adapted from a tale told by Andrew Lang in The Animal Story Book, which was originally published by Longmans, Green And Co., London & New York, in 1896. This part of the story of Bucephalus is taken from Plutarch.

Andrew Lang (1844–1912) was a Scottish poet, novelist, literary critic, and folklorist best known for his influential work in collecting and popularizing folk and fairy tales from around the world. He is most famous for the Coloured Fairy Books series, beginning with The Blue Fairy Book in 1889, which gathered traditional stories from various cultures into accessible volumes for children and families.

There are not so many stories about horses as there are about dogs and cats, yet almost every great general has had his favourite horse, who has gone with him through many campaigns and borne him safe on many battle-fields. At a town in Sicily called Agrigentum, they set such store by their horses, that pyramids were raised over their burial-place, and the Emperor Augustus built a splendid monument over the grave of an old favourite.

The most famous horse, perhaps, who ever lived, was one belonging to Alexander the Great, and was called Bucephalus. When the king was a boy, Bucephalus was brought before Philip, King of Macedon, Alexander's father, by Philonicus the Thessalian, and offered for sale for the large sum of thirteen talents. Beautiful though he was, Philip wisely declined to buy him before knowing what manner of horse he was, and ordered him to be led into a neighbouring field, and a groom to mount him. But it was in vain that the best and most experienced riders approached the horse. He reared up on his hind legs, and would suffer none to come near him. So Philonicus the Thessalian was told to take his horse back where he came from, for the king would have none of him.

Now the boy Alexander stood by, and his heart went out to the beautiful creature. And he cried out, "What a good horse we lose for lack of skill to mount him!"

Philip the king heard these words, and his soul was vexed to see the horse depart, but he did not know what else to do. Then he turned to Alexander and said, "Do you think that you, young and untried, can ride this horse better than those who have grown old in the stables?"

To which Alexander made answer, "This horse I know I could ride better than they."

"And if you fail," asked Philip, "what price will you pay for your good conceit of yourself?"

And Alexander laughed out and said gaily, "I will pay the price of the horse."

And thus it was settled.

So Alexander drew near to the horse, and took him by the bridle, turning his face to the sun so that he might not be frightened at the movements of his own shadow, for the prince had noticed that it scared him greatly. Then Alexander stroked his head and led him forwards, feeling his temper all the while, and when the horse began to get uneasy, the prince suddenly leapt on his back, and gradually curbed him with the bridle. Suddenly, as Bucephalus gave up trying to throw his rider, and only pawed the ground impatient to be off, Alexander shook the reins, and bidding him go, they flew like lightning round the course. This was Alexander's first conquest, and as he jumped down from the horse, his father exclaimed, "Go, my son, and seek a kingdom that is worthy, for Macedon is too small for such as you."

Henceforth Bucephalus made it clear that he served Alexander and no one else. He would submit quietly to having the trappings of a king's steed fastened on his head, and the royal saddle put on, but if any groom tried to mount him, back would go his ears and up would go his heels, and none dared come near him. For ten years after Alexander succeeded his father on the throne of Macedon (B.C. 336), Bucephalus bore him through all his battles, and was, says Pliny, "of a passing good and memorable service in the wars," and even when wounded, as he once was at the taking of Thebes, would not suffer his master to mount another horse. Together these two swam rivers, crossed mountains, penetrated into the dominions of the Great King, and farther still into the heart of Asia, beyond the Caspian and the river Oxus, where no European army had gone before. Then turning sharp south, he crossed the range of the Hindu Kush, and entering the country of the Five Rivers, he prepared to attack Porus, king of India. But age and the wanderings of ten years had worn Bucephalus out. After one last victory near the Hydaspes or Jhelum, the old horse sank down and died, full of years and honours.

Bitter were the lamentations of the king for the friend of his childhood, but his grief did not show itself only in weeping. The most splendid funeral Alexander could devise was given to Bucephalus, and a gorgeous tomb erected over his body. And more than that, Alexander resolved that the memory of his old horse should be kept green in these burning Indian deserts, thousands of miles from the Thessalian plains where he was born, so round his tomb the king built a city, and it was called Bucephalia.

The Hooves of Heaven

A Chinese Tale

This is my own version of a traditional legend, written and adapted from various sources and historical notes in my collection of folk and fairy tales. The Hooves of Heaven originates in stories surrounding Emperor Wu of Han (Han Wudi, r. 141–87 BCE) and his quest for supernatural horses. In Chinese legend and early historical texts such as Shiji (Records of the Grand Historian), Emperor Wu longed for the "Heavenly Horses" (Tianma) said to dwell in the lands of Ferghana, far to the west.

In folktale form, "The Hooves of Heaven" blends history with myth: the emperor is not just seeking faster mounts but striving for a bridge between the mortal world and the divine, with horses whose very hooves echoed the thunder of the heavens.

In the twilight of the Han Dynasty, when maps were drawn in ink but expanded in blood, the Son of Heaven dreamt of horses that walked the sky.

Emperor Wu of Han, a man who spoke to the stars and hunted omens in tea leaves, stood one night on the stone balcony of his palace, gazing into a sky bruised with moonlight. He had grown weary of slow-footed steeds that could not cross deserts or catch up with fleeing barbarian scouts. He longed for something divine, for horses not born of earth but of cloud and fire.

In his dream, they had wings. Their manes flowed like banners in a storm, their hooves struck thunder, and their eyes were orbs of pale gold. When they galloped, the air itself split. When they neighed, mountains trembled. He awoke whispering a name that the stars had poured into his ears.

"Tianma. Heavenly Horses."

And so he sent an envoy westward, past the Jade Gates, past the bones of merchants in the sand, past kingdoms with foreign tongues and sun-darkened faces. This man was named Zhang Qian, a general with a diplomat's smile and a spy's patience.

Zhang Qian walked a road lined with betrayal. He passed through Dayuan, the Kingdom of Ferghana, where it was whispered that divine horses grazed on silver grass, drank only mountain spring water, and left no dung behind. These were no ordinary beasts.

"They sweat blood," one trader muttered over spiced wine.

"Because they drink from copper-veined springs," said another.

"No," said an old woman with a hawk feather in her braid. "Because they are not of this world."

And Zhang Qian believed.

He returned not only with scrolls and spices but with a vision for war. The Emperor listened and wept, for greed, for glory, or perhaps awe, and decreed, "Bring me the Tianma. They shall pull the chariots of heaven and trample my enemies beneath their silver hooves."

But the horses were guarded jealously. The Kingdom of Ferghana refused to part with them. They worshipped them, fed them apples dipped in honey, and sang lullabies to them in Sanskrit. Their people believed the Tianma were left by the gods after a forgotten war between Heaven and Earth.

So Emperor Wu sent armies. Not once, but twice. The first campaign failed. The weather turned to snow and ice and soldiers died clawing at mountain passes. The second bled gold and flame. Cities burned. Wells were poisoned. And finally, Ferghana yielded, reluctantly, bitterly.

In the end they had no choice, but they gave only the weakest of the Tianma to the Emperor, and in small number. It was enough to call it tribute, and just enough to haunt the Emperor's dreams further.

The horses arrived in Luoyang in cages of sandalwood, their wings clipped, not literally, but with weariness. Yet even in captivity, they were radiant. One of them refused food and died with a defiant cry that cracked a window in the palace. Another shattered its hooves against marble and still outpaced the imperial guards before collapsing. A third grew tame and allowed only the Emperor himself to touch it.

And then, one spring morning, the impossible happened. It leapt. Not over a fence. Not across a field. Into the sky.

Witnesses say it unfurled wings of fire, translucent and veined with starlight, like a butterfly the size of a pavilion. It rose above the Forbidden City, circled the golden roofs, and vanished into the east.

Priests called it a celestial sign. Scholars argued about physics. Farmers dropped to their knees. And the Emperor, old and trembling, whispered again, "Tianma."

He wept not for the horse, but for the idea of the horse, and for what it represented. For the emperor the Tianma signified victory of vision over bone, and the possibility of the divine entering the realm of men.

He would never see another Tianma fly. But he ordered their image carved into every shield, and into every imperial standard. The army of Han would ride beneath their wings, even if only in symbol.

The scholars say the Tianma that flew east never touched ground again. It soared into clouds, found a rift between the layers of sky, and slipped into the Palace of the Moon. The goddess Chang'e saw it and wept for joy, for even immortals grow lonely. At times the Tianma can be seen galloping along the Milky Way, chasing the lovers Zhinü and Niulang, protecting them from the wrath of the Jade Emperor.

And to this day, on certain nights, when the wind is warm and the stars breathe like embers, you can see a horse-shaped constellation above the mountains of Central Asia. Farmers call it the Sky-Hooved One.

Pegasus, The Winged Horse

A Greek Tale

This story has been substantially adapted from a tale told by William Patten in The Junior Classics, Volume 3: Tales from Greece and Rome, which was originally published by P. F. Collier & Son, New York, in 1912. This version of the tales was originally presented by Nathaniel Hawthorne.

Nathaniel Hawthorne (1804–1864) was a prominent American novelist, short story writer, and classicist best known for his dark romanticism and richly symbolic prose. Though most famous for works like The Scarlet Letter and The House of the Seven Gables, he also had a deep interest in classical antiquity, mythology, and moral allegory. His classical knowledge informed much of his writing, especially in his retellings of Greek myths for younger audiences in A Wonder-Book for Girls and Boys and Tanglewood Tales.

Long ago, in the hills of ancient Greece, a fountain burst from the earth and sparkled in the sunlight. This was the Fountain of Pirene, a place of legend and beauty. One golden afternoon, a young man named Bellerophon arrived at the fountain. He was handsome, strong, and carried in his hand a gleaming bridle decorated with jewels and gold.

By the water, he met an old man, a middle-aged farmer, a little boy, and a young woman filling her pitcher. He politely asked the maiden if he could have a drink from the fountain, and she smiled and told him its name, Pirene. She explained that it was named after a woman who, long ago, wept so bitterly over the death of her son that she turned into a spring. The water, she said, was her endless tears.

As Bellerophon drank, the farmer noticed the fancy bridle and joked, "You must've lost a mighty fine horse to be carrying that around."

Bellerophon smiled. "I'm searching for a horse, but not just any horse. I've come to find Pegasus, the winged steed said to drink from this very fountain."

The farmer laughed out loud. "Wings? On a horse? That's nonsense!"

Even the old man, leaning on his staff, could barely remember ever seeing such a thing. But the young woman once thought she saw something in the sky, either a great bird or a winged horse. And the little boy, wide-eyed and honest, said he saw Pegasus all the time, reflected in the water or heard his neigh echo through the hills.

Bellerophon listened to the boy. He believed in Pegasus and stayed by the fountain for days, waiting. Many mocked him. Some called him foolish, while others tried to buy his bridle, but Bellerophon never gave up hope. Each morning, the little boy returned, certain that today would be the day. And finally, it was.

From the sky, a blur of silver wings circled downward. Pegasus, wild and radiant, landed by the fountain and drank. Bellerophon held his breath, then leapt from the bushes and, in one swift motion, placed the bridle on the horse's head. Pegasus reared and tried to shake him off, soaring into the clouds, diving and twisting, but Bellerophon held on. When the bit was finally in place, the mighty horse stilled. They looked at each other, and in that moment, trust was born.

They became companions. Together, they flew across mountains and seas. But Bellerophon had a duty, and that was to slay the Chimera, a monstrous creature with a lion's head, a goat's head, and a serpent's tail, breathing fire and destruction across the land of Lycia.

Riding Pegasus, Bellerophon soared into battle. They dove from the clouds as the Chimera spewed flame. Dodging fire and claws, Bellerophon struck. One head fell, then another. Finally, with a mighty cry and one last dive, he plunged his sword into the monster's heart, and the Chimera fell, burning, from the sky, never to rise again.

Victorious, Bellerophon returned to the fountain, where the villagers watched in awe. The boy was there, waiting, his eyes filled with wonder. "You did it," he whispered.

But Bellerophon shook his head. "No…we did it."

And as a sign of love and freedom, Bellerophon unbuckled the bridle and whispered to Pegasus, "You are free."

But the winged horse stayed by his side, not out of command, but out of friendship.

Story Of The Race Between The Elephant And The Horses

An Indian Tale

This story has been adapted from a tale told by Somadeva Bhatta in The Kathá Sarit Ságara, this version being published by Baptist Mission Press in 1884.

Somadeva Bhatta was an 11th-century Kashmiri poet and scholar best known for compiling the Kathā-saritsāgara ("Ocean of the Streams of Story"), one of the largest and most influential collections of Indian tales. Written in Sanskrit verse, this vast compendium draws on earlier sources, particularly the now-lost Bṛhatkathā by Guṇāḍhya, and contains an intricate web of stories within stories, including folktales, legends, fables, and moral parables. Somadeva composed the work during a time of political instability in Kashmir, possibly to entertain and console Queen Suryamati, the consort of King Ananta.

One day, when Naraváhanadatta was in the garden, two brothers, who were princes, and who had come from a foreign land, suddenly paid him a visit. He received them cordially, and they bowed before him, and one of them said to him, "We are the sons by different mothers of a king in the city of Vaisákha. My name is Ruchiradeva and the name of this brother of mine is Potraka. I have a swift female elephant, and he has two horses. And a dispute has arisen between us about them. I say that the elephant is the fleetest, while he maintains that his horses are both faster. I have agreed that if I lose the race, I am to surrender the elephant, but if he loses, he is to give me both his horses. Now no one but you is fit to be a judge of their relative speed, so come to my house, my lord, and preside over this trial. Accede to our request. For you are the wishing-tree that grants all petitions, and we have come from afar to petition you about this matter."

When Naraváhanadatta received this invitation from Ruchiradeva, he consented out of good nature, and out of the interest he took in the elephant and the horses. He set out in a chariot drawn by swift horses, which the brothers had brought, and they all reached the city of Vaisákha.

When he entered that splendid city, the ladies, bewildered and excited, beheld him with eyes the lashes of which were turned up, and made these comments on him, "Who can this be? Can it be the god of Love new-created from his ashes without Rati? Or a second moon roaming through the heaven without a spot on its surface? Or an arrow of desire made by the Creator, in the form of a man, for the sudden complete overthrow of the female heart."

Then Naraváhanadatta beheld the lovely temple of the god of Love, whose worship had been established there by men of older times. He entered and worshipped that god, the source of supreme felicity, and rested for a moment, and shook off the fatigue of the journey. Then he entered as a friend the house of Ruchiradeva, which was near that temple, and was honoured by being made to walk in front of him. He was delighted at the sight of that magnificent palace, full of splendid horses and elephants, which was in a state of rejoicing on account of his visit.

There he was entertained with various hospitalities by Ruchiradeva, and there he beheld his sister of splendid beauty. Naraváhanadatta's mind and his eyes were so captivated by her glorious beauty, that he forgot all about his absence from home and his separation from his family. She too threw lovingly upon him her expanded eye, which resembled a garland of full blown blue lotuses, and so chose him as her husband. Her name was Jayendrasená, and he thought so much upon her that the goddess of sleep did not take possession of him at night, just as much less did other females.

The next day Potraka brought that pair of horses equal to the wind in swiftness; but Ruchiradeva, who was skilled in all the secrets of the art of driving, himself mounted the female elephant, and partly by the animal's natural speed, partly by his dexterity in urging it on, beat them in the race.

When Ruchiradeva had beaten those two splendid horses, the son of the king of Vatsa entered the palace, and at that very moment a messenger arrived from his father. The messenger, when he saw Naraváhanadatta, fell at his feet, and said, "The king, hearing from your retinue that you have come here, has sent me to you with this message. 'How comes it that you have gone so far from the garden without letting me know? I am impatient for your return, so abandon the diversion that occupies your attention, and return quickly.'"

When he heard this message from his father's messenger, Naraváhanadatta, who was also intent on obtaining the object of his flame, was in a state of perplexity.

And at that very moment a merchant, in a great state of delight, came, bowing at a distance, and praised that prince, saying, "Victory to you, O you god of love without the flowery bow! Victory to you, O Lord, the future emperor of the Vidyádharas! Were you not seen to be charming as a boy, and when growing up, the terror of your foes? So surely the gods shall behold you like Vishnu, striding victorious over the heaven, conquering Bali."

With these and other praises the great merchant magnified the prince, then having been honoured by him, he proceeded at his request to tell the story of his life.

Virgil And The Bronze Horse

A Roman Tale

This tale has been adapted from an original by Charles Godfrey Leland in his book, The Unpublished Legends of Virgil, published by Elliot Stock, London, in 1899.

Charles Godfrey Leland (1824–1903) was an American writer, journalist, folklorist, and amateur anthropologist best known for his studies of folklore, especially that of marginalised or "outsider" cultures. Fluent in multiple languages and deeply curious about folk traditions, Leland collected and published stories, songs, and customs from the Romani people (notably in The Gypsies and The English Gypsies and Their Language), and Italian witches and peasants.

One day Virgil went to visit the Emperor, and not finding him in his usual good temper, asked what the matter was, adding that he hoped it would be in his power to do something to relieve him.

Then the Emperor complained that what troubled him was that all his horses seemed to be ill or bewitched, behaving like wild beasts, or as if evil spirits were in them, and what which grieved him most was that his favourite white horse was most afflicted of all.

"Do not vex yourself for such a thing," replied Virgil. "I will cure your horses and all the others in the city."

Then he caused to be made a beautiful horse of bronze, and it was so well made that no one, unless by the will of Virgil could have made the like. And whenever a horse which suffered in any way beheld it, the animal was at once cured.

All the smiths and horse-doctors in Rome were greatly angered at this, because after Virgil made the bronze horse they had nothing to do. So they planned to revenge themselves on him. They all assembled in a vile place frequented by thieves and assassins, and there agreed to kill Virgil. Going to his house by night, they looked for him, but he escaped, so they, finding the bronze horse, broke it to pieces, and then fled.

When Virgil returned and found the horse in fragments he was greatly grieved, and said, "The smiths have done this. However, I will yet do some good with the metal, for I will make from it a bell; and when the smiths hear it ring, I will give them a peal to remember me by."

So the bell was made and given to the Church of San Martino. And the first time it was tolled it sang:

"I was a horse of bronze, and tall.

My enemies broke me to pieces small.

But a friend who loves me well

Had me made into a bell.

Now here on high I proudly ring,

And as I ding-dong, ding-dong sing,

I tell aloud, as I toll and wave,

Who is a wittol and a knave."

And all the smiths who had broken the horse when they heard the bell became as deaf as posts. Then great remorse came over them and shame, and they threw themselves down on the ground before Virgil and begged his pardon.

Virgil replied, "I pardon you, but for a penance you must have six other bells made to add to this, to make a peal, and put them all in the same church."

This they did, and then regained their hearing.

The Song of Hayagrīva

An Indian Tale

This is my own version of a traditional legend, written and adapted from various sources and historical notes in my collection of folk and fairy tales. The Song of Hayagrīva comes from Hindu and Buddhist traditions of South Asia, where Hayagrīva ("Horse-Necked" or "Horse-Headed") is a divine being associated with wisdom, protection, and sacred knowledge.

Based on those origins, the tale also saw later strong development in Tibetan and Himalayan Buddhism, where it became both a myth and a living religious hymn tradition.

In the age before memory, before even the stars had names, there was only silence. And in that silence, knowledge lay sleeping. When the world was still new and wisdom was as fragile as dew upon a leaf, the Vedas, the sacred breath of creation, were stolen.

The demons, the Daityas, born of ambition and shadow, rose from the oceanic depths. Led by two brothers, Madhu and Kaitabha, they moved through the ether with wings of fire

229

and deceit. Their hearts were forged of arrogance, and their fingers longed to twist the threads of the cosmos.

From the very lips of Brahma, who sat upon his lotus above the waters of time, they snatched the four Vedas, Rig, Sama, Yajur, Atharva, tearing them from his tongue like thieves stealing the sun from the sky.

Brahma cried out in fear, for without the Vedas, the world would spiral into unknowing. Fire would forget to burn, water would forget to flow, and man would forget his own name. He turned his eyes to the heavens, seeking the Preserver.

Far away, in the sleeping folds of the cosmic ocean, Vishnu lay in yogic slumber upon the coiled body of Ananta-Shesha, the infinite serpent. His breath was the wind between stars. From his navel bloomed a golden lotus upon which Brahma sat, but Vishnu himself slept, dreamless.

Brahma, trembling, approached the dreamer. "O Lord of All That Wakes and Sleeps," he pleaded. "The Vedas are gone, stolen by those who would use them to unmake the world. If knowledge fades, there will be no prayer, no purpose, no path."

But Vishnu did not stir.

The cosmos held its breath. Then, from the silence came a sound, unlike any other. It was neither roar nor whisper. It was the sharp cry of a horse, echoing across all planes of existence.

In that moment, Vishnu stirred. But he did not rise as before, in his usual divine form with four arms and serene eyes. No.

This time he rose as Hayagrīva, the horse-headed god, his mane like comet-fire, his eyes like thunderclouds, his neck coiled with galaxies. His body gleamed like bronze in the first dawn. His voice was both human and beast, terrible and tender.

Vishnu chose the horse form because the horse is sacred, because the horse is swift, noble, and unafraid of the dark, because knowledge, like the gallop of a steed, must never stop moving forward. With sword in hand, Hayagrīva pierced the veil between worlds and descended.

The demons had taken refuge in Patala, the underworld realm of illusions and serpents. There, they sang the Vedas backwards, twisting mantras into curses, and unravelling order into chaos.

Madhu and Kaitabha sat upon thrones of bone, intoxicated by stolen truths, laughing as the laws of the universe bent around them. They had learned too much, too quickly, and had become drunk on power. But they did not expect the coming of Hayagrīva.

He came not with armies, but alone. Not with thunder, but with silence. His hooves struck the ground with purpose. His breath scattered the illusions of Patala like autumn leaves. Where he walked, darkness retreated.

Madhu raised a trident and Kaitabha called upon cursed winds. But Hayagrīva was knowledge incarnate. And knowledge is a blade that no ignorance can parry. With a cry that split mountains, Hayagrīva struck down Madhu. With a gaze that melted illusions, he silenced Kaitabha. From their crumbling thrones, he retrieved the Vedas, each glowing with a voice, a rhythm, a memory. He held them close, not as weapons, but as children lost and found.

Hayagrīva ascended once more, riding the winds of thought, his mane trailing verses. When he reached the edge of time, he did not speak, he sang, he sang the Vedas back into the world. And wherever his voice touched, creation remembered itself.

The fire rekindled.

The rivers returned to their banks.

The birds remembered their songs.

And man, opening his eyes at dawn, whispered a prayer without knowing why.

Hayagrīva did not remain long in horse form. As swiftly as he came, he dissolved back into the dream of Vishnu, returning to the deep breath beneath all things. But the horse's cry still echoes in meditation, in the gallop of a wild idea, in the moment you remember something ancient that you never learned.

Hayagrīva became more than a god. He became a symbol. Hayagrīva is the keeper of wisdom. Hayagrīva is the guardian of sacred words. Hayagrīva is the divine whisper that rides the wind.

"Let knowledge rise as Hayagrīva rose,

fierce, pure, and unafraid of the dark."

The Story Of The Half-Man-Riding-On-The-Worse-Half-Of-A-Lame-Horse

A Romanian Tale

This tale has been adapted from an original by Ignácz Kúnos in his book, Turkish Fairy Tales And Folk Tales, published by A. H. Bullen, London, in 1901.

Ignácz Kúnos (1860–1945) was a Hungarian linguist, ethnographer, and folklorist best known for his extensive work collecting and publishing Turkish and Anatolian folk tales.

Once upon a time, long long ago, in the days when poplars bore pears and rushes violets, when bears could switch themselves with their tails like cows, and wolves and lambs kissed and cuddled each other, there lived an Emperor whose hair was already white, and who yet had no son to bless himself with. The poor Emperor would have given anything to have had a little son of his own like other men, but all his wishes were in vain.

At last, when he was quite an old man, Fortune took pity on him, and a darling boy was born to him, the like of which the world had never seen before. The Emperor gave him the name of Aleodor, and gathered east and west, north and south, together to rejoice in his joy at the child's christening. The revels lasted three days and three nights, and all the guests who made merry there with the Emperor could think of nothing else for the rest of their lives.

The lad grew up as strong as an oak and as lovely as a rose, while his father the Emperor drew nearer every day to the edge of the grave, and when the hour of his death arrived he took the child on his knees and said to him, "My darling son, behold the Lord calls me. The moment is at hand when I am to share the common lot of man. I foresee that you will become a great man, and though I be dead my bones will rejoice in the tomb at your noble deeds. As to the administration of this realm I need tell you nothing, for you, with your wisdom, will know how it behoves a king to rule. One thing there is, nevertheless, that I must tell you. Do you see that mountain over yonder? Beware of ever setting your foot upon it, for 'twill be to your hurt and harm. That mountain belongs to the 'Half-man-riding-on-the-worse-half-of-a-lame-horse,' and whosoever ventures upon that mountain cannot escape unscathed."

He had no sooner said these words than his throat rattled three times, and he gave up the ghost. He departed to his place like every other human soul that is born into the world, though there was never Emperor like him since the world began. All those of his household and court mourned him.

Aleodor, from the moment that he ascended the throne, ruled the land wisely like a mature statesman, though in age he was but a child. All the world delighted in his sway, and men thanked Heaven for allowing them to live in the days of such a prince.

All the time that was not taken up by affairs of State, Aleodor spent in the chase. But he always bore in mind the precepts of his father, and took care not to exceed the bounds which had been set him.

One day, however he fell into a brown study, and never noticed that he had overstepped the domains of the Half-man till, after taking a dozen steps or so onwards, he found himself face to face with the monster. That he was trespassing on the grounds of this stunted and terrible creature did not trouble him over-much, it was the thought that he had transgressed the dying command of his dear father that grieved him.

"Ho, ho!" cried the hideous monster, "do you not know that every scoundrel who oversteps my bounds becomes my property?"

"Yes," replied Aleodor, "but I must tell you that it was through want of thought and without wishing it that I have trodden on your ground. Against you I have no evil design at all."

"I know better than that," replied the monster, "but I see that, like all cowards, you think it best to make excuses."

"No, so sure as God preserves me, I am no coward. I have told you the simple truth, but if you would fight, I am ready. Choose your weapons! Shall we slash with sabres, or slog with clubs, or wrestle together?"

"Neither the one nor the other," replied the monster. "One way only can you escape your just punishment. You must fetch me the daughter of the Green Emperor!"

Aleodor would very much have liked to have got out of the difficulty some other way, as affairs of State would not allow him to take so long a journey, a journey on which he could find no guide to direct him, but what did the monster know of all that? Aleodor felt that if he would avoid the shame of being thought a robber and a trampler on the rights of others, he must indeed find the daughter of the Green Emperor. Besides, he wanted to escape with a whole skin if he could; so at last he promised that he would do the service required of him.

Now the Half-man-riding-on-the-worse-half-of-a-lame-horse knew very well that, as a man of honour, Aleodor would never depart from his plighted word, so he said to him, "Go now, in God's name, and may good luck attend you!"

So Aleodor departed. He went on and on, thinking over and over again how he was to accomplish his task, and so keep his word, when he came to the margin of a pond, and there he saw a pike dashing its life out on the shore. He immediately went up to it to satisfy his hunger with it, when the pike said to him, "Slay me not, Boy-Beautiful, but cast me rather back into the water again, and then I will do you good whenever you think of me."

Aleodor listened to the pike, and threw it back into the water again. Then the pike said to him again, "Take this scale, and whenever you look at it and think of me I will be with you."

Then the youth went on further and marvelled greatly at such a strange encounter.

Presently he fell in with a crow that had one wing broken. He would have killed the crow and eaten it, but the crow said to him, "Boy-Beautiful, Boy-Beautiful, why will you burden your soul on my account? Far better would it be e if you bind up my wing, and much good will I return for you with for your kindness."

Aleodor listened, for his heart was as kind as his hand was cunning, and he bound up the crow's wing. When he made ready to go on again, the crow said to him, "Take this feather, you gallant youth, and whenever you look at it and think of me, I will be with you."

Then Aleodor took the feather and went on his way. He hadn't gone a hundred paces further when he stumbled upon an ant. He would have trodden upon it, when the ant said to him, "Spare my life, O Emperor Aleodor, and I'll deliver you also from death! Take this little bit of membrane from my wing, and whenever you think of me, I'll be with you."

When Aleodor heard these words, and how the ant called him by his name, he raised his foot again and let the ant go where it would. He also went on his way, and after journeying for many days he came at last to the palace of the Green Emperor. There he knocked at the door, and stood waiting for someone to come out and ask him what he wanted.

He stood there one day, he stood there two days, but as for anyone coming out to ask him what he wanted, there was no sign of it. When the third day dawned, however, the Green Emperor called to his servants and gave them a talking to that they were likely to remember. "How comes it," said he, "that a man should be standing at my gates three days without anyone going out to ask him what he wants? Is this what I pay you wages for?"

The servants of the Green Emperor looked up, and they looked down, but they had not one word to say for themselves. At last they went and called Aleodor and led him before the Emperor.

"What do you want, my son?" inquired the Emperor, "and why were you waiting at the gates of my court?"

"I have come, great Emperor, to seek your daughter."

"Good, my son. But, first of all, we must make a compact together, for such is the custom of my court. You must hide yourself wherever you will three times running. If my daughter finds you all three times, your head shall be struck off and stuck on a stake, the only one out of a hundred that has not a suitor's head upon it. But if she does not find you three times, you shall have her from me with all imperial courtesy."

"My hope, great Emperor, is in the Lord, who will not allow me to perish. We will put something else on this stake of yours, but not the head of a man. Let us make the compact."

"You agree?"

"I agree."

So they made a compact, and the deeds were drawn out and signed and sealed.

Then the daughter of the Emperor met him next day, and it was arranged that he should hide himself as best he could.

But now he was in an agony that tortured him worse than death, for he wondered again and again where and how he could best hide himself, for nothing less than his head was at stake. And as he kept walking about, and brooding and pondering, he remembered the pike. Then he took out the fish's scale, looked at it, and thought of the fish's master, and immediately, the pike stood before him and said, "What do you want of me, Boy-Beautiful?"

"What do I want? You may well ask that! Look what has happened to me! Can you tell me what to do?"

"That is your business no longer. Leave it to me!"

And immediately striking Aleodor with his tail, he turned him into a little shell-fish, and hid him among the other little shell-fish at the bottom of the sea.

When the damsel appeared, she put on her eye-glass and looked for him in every direction, but could see him nowhere. Her other wooers had hidden themselves in caves, or behind houses, or under haycocks and haystacks, or in some hole or corner, but Aleodor hid himself in such a way that the damsel began to fear that she would be vanquished. Then it occurred to her to turn her eye-glass towards the sea, and she saw him beneath a heap of mussels, for her eye-glass was a magic eye-glass.

"I see you, you rascal," cried she, "how you have bothered me, to be sure! From being a man you have made yourself a mussel, and hidden at the bottom of the sea."

This he couldn't deny, so of course he had to come up again.

But she said to the Emperor, "I think, dear father, this youth will suit me. He is nice and comely. Even if I find him all three times let me have him, for he is not stupid like the others. Why, you can see from his figure even how different he is."

"We shall see," replied the Emperor.

On the second day Aleodor thought about the crow, and immediately the crow stood before him, and said to him, "What do you want, my master?"

"Look now, senseless one, at what has happened to me. Can you show me a way out of it?"

"Let us try!" and with that it struck him with its wing and turned him into a young crow, and placed him in the midst of a flock of crows that were flying high in the air in the teeth of a fierce tempest.

Then the damsel came again with her eye-glass and searched for him in every direction. He was nowhere to be found. She looked for him on the earth, but he was not there. She looked for him in the rivers and in the sea, but he was not there. The damsel grew pensive. She searched and searched till mid-day, when it occurred to her to look upwards also. And perceiving him in the glory of the sky in the midst of a swarm of crows, she pointed him out with her finger and cried, "Look! look! Rogue that you are! Come down from there, O man, that has made yourself into a bit of a bird! Nothing in the fields of heaven can escape my eye!"

Then he came down, for what else could he do? Even the Emperor himself now began to be amazed at the skill and cunning of Aleodor, and lent an ear to the prayers of his daughter. Inasmuch, however, as the compact declared that Aleodor was to hide three times, the Emperor said to his daughter, "Wait once more, for I am curious to see what place he will find to hide himself in next."

The third day, early in the morning, he thought of the ant, and the ant was immediately by his side. When she had found out what he wanted she said to him, "Leave it to me, and if she find you I am here to help you."

So the ant turned him into a flower-seed, and hid him in the very skirts of the damsel's dress without her perceiving it.

Then the Emperor's daughter rose up, took her eye-glass, and sought for him all day long, but look where she would, she could not find him. She plagued herself almost to death in her search, for she felt that he was close at hand, though see him she could not. She looked through her eye-glass on the ground, and in the sea, and up in the sky, but she could see him nowhere, and towards evening, tired out by so much searching, she exclaimed, "Show yourself then, this once! I feel that you are close at hand, and yet I cannot see you. You have conquered, and I am yours."

Then when he heard her say that he had conquered, he slipped slowly down from her skirts and revealed himself. The Emperor had now nothing more to say, so he gave the youth his daughter, and when they departed, he escorted them to the boundaries of his empire with great pomp and ceremony.

While they were on the road they stopped at a place to rest, and after they had refreshed themselves somewhat with food, he laid his head in her lap and fell asleep. The daughter of the

Emperor could not resist looking at him, and her eyes filled with tears as they feasted on his comeliness and beauty. Then her heart grew soft within her, and she could not help kissing him. But Aleodor, when he awoke, gave her a buffet with the palm of his hand that awoke the echoes.

"No but, my dear Aleodor!" cried she, "you have indeed a heavy hand."

"I have slapped you," said he, "for the deed you have done, for I have not taken you for myself, but for him who bade me seek you."

"Good, my brother, but why did you not tell me so at home? for then I also would have known what to do. But let be now, for all that is past."

Then they set out again till they came alive and well to the Half-man-riding-on-the-worse-half-of-a-lame-horse.

"Lo, now! I have done my service," said Aleodor, and with that he would have departed. But when the girl beheld the monster, she shivered with disgust, and would not stay with him for a single moment. The hideous cripple drew near to the maiden, and began to caress her with honeyed words, so she might go with him willingly. But the girl said to him, "Depart from me, Satan, and go to your mother Hell, who has cast you upon the face of the earth!"

Then the half-monster half-man was near to melting for the love he had for the damsel, and, writhing away on his belly, he fetched his mother that she might help to persuade the maid to be his wife. But meanwhile the damsel had dug a little trench all round her, and stood rooted to the spot with her eyes fixed on the ground. The hideous satanic skeleton of a monster could not get at her.

"Depart from the face of the earth, you abomination!" cried she, "the world is well rid of such a pestilential monster as you."

Still he strove and strove to get at her, but finding at last he could not reach her, he burst with rage and fury that a mere woman should have so covered him with shame and reproach.

Then Aleodor added the domain of the Half-man-riding-on-the-worse-half-of-a-lame-horse to his own possessions, took the daughter of the Green Emperor to wife, and returned to his own empire. And when his people saw him coming back in the company of a smiling spouse as beautiful as the stars of heaven, they welcomed him with great joy, and, mounting once more his imperial throne, he ruled his people in peace and plenty till the day of his death.

The Horse And His Rider

A Turkish Tale

This tale is my version of an original tale by Epiphanius Wilson in his book, Turkish Literature, published by P. F. Collier & Son, New York, in 1901.

Epiphanius Wilson (1845–1916) was a prolific American editor, translator, and scholar best known for compiling and translating a wide array of world literature into English during the late 19th and early 20th centuries. His work focused on making global literary traditions, particularly classical, Eastern, and religious texts, accessible to Western audiences. He edited and translated texts from Sanskrit, Chinese, Arabic, Greek, Latin, and other languages, often adapting or abridging them for general readers.

Long ago, when the sun was kinder and the mountains still whispered to the clouds, there lived a proud and splendid horse on the edge of an Anatolian village. His coat gleamed like brushed bronze in the morning light, and his mane rippled like silk in the wind. He was strong of limb, swift of foot, and clever enough to know it.

This horse belonged to a rider, a man who was neither wealthy nor famous, but who treated his steed with a quiet but firm kindness. Every morning, he would rise before the muezzin's call and feed the horse with clean oats and fresh water from the well. He would brush the dust from his coat and speak to him softly before fitting the bridle and saddle. They would ride together into the fields, or to market, or sometimes even into the wild, rocky hills where wolves howled beneath the stars.

But the horse, though well-fed and well-kept, grew restless in his heart. One evening, as the rider rubbed balm into a sore on his leg, the horse turned his dark eyes toward the man and spoke.

"Master," he said, for in those days beasts and men still spoke to one another when the air was clear and hearts were honest, "tell me, how is it fair that a creature such as I, born with strength and grace and the wind in my lungs, should bow his back to carry one as small and feeble as you?"

The rider looked up, surprised but calm. He set aside the balm and sat beside the horse, stroking his mane as he replied. "You speak true. You are strong, and swift, and noble. But I feed you with care, give you shelter from rain and sun, and guide you to water and pasture. Have I ever struck you without cause? Have I ever led you into hunger?"

"But you bind my head with leather and metal," said the horse, shaking his bridle. "You place weight on my back and demand I run, even when I am tired. You ride me through cold winds and stony ground. And worst of all, you steal my freedom."

The rider was silent a long time, then stood and removed the bit from the horse's mouth. He took off the saddle and the reins, and stepped back.

"Then go," he said, his voice heavy. "Claim your freedom, noble one. The world is wide."

The horse wasted no time. With a proud snort, he tossed his mane and galloped off into the wild hills, where the grass grew tall and sweet, and cool water ran in silver threads through the gullies. There he lived without burden. No saddle pressed his back, no hand tugged his bridle. He ate when he wished, drank when he pleased, and slept beneath the stars, a king of the wild places.

Days passed, then weeks. His muscles grew round with ease. His belly filled out from the lush grasses. Birds rested on his back, unafraid, and even the wind seemed to part for him. But freedom, as it does, came with its shadows.

One cold dawn, while dew still clung to the grass, a pack of wolves caught his scent. These were no frightened village dogs, but lean, silent hunters of the high places, with eyes like polished stone, their breath steaming in the morning chill. They had watched him grow fat. They had seen how he no longer galloped like the wind, but lumbered like a cart horse.

The chase began.

At first, the horse ran like lightning. Rocks flew from his hooves, and his mane streamed behind him. The wolves howled but could not catch him. But the hills were long, and the fat beneath his skin weighed him down. His breath came in gasps. His hooves slipped on damp stones. The wolves gained ground, slowly, steadily, until their snarling jaws were at his heels. He tried to scream, but only a ragged whinny came. A fang caught his flank. Then another. He stumbled. He fell.

And as the wolves tore at him, the horse cried out, not to the stars, nor to the mountains, but to the memory of the rider who had once fed him with careful hands and shielded him from storms.

"Oh master!" he gasped with his final breath. "Your bit was gentler than their fangs! Your weight was lighter than this fate!"

Thus perished the proud horse who mistook care for cruelty, and burden for bondage.

And so the tale teaches us that to live in the world is to bear some load, be it duty, labour, or love. Those who mistake guidance for chains may find that freedom, when taken without wisdom, can lead not to peace, but to peril. For even in liberty, the wolf waits.

Pomo And The Goblin Horse

A Tuscan Tale

This tale is my version of an original tale by Isabella Mary Anderton in her book, Tuscan Folk-Lore And Sketches, published by Arnold |Fairbairns, London, in 1905.

Isabella Mary Anderton (1854–1926) was a British writer, folklorist, and classical scholar known for her translations and retellings of ancient legends and folk tales, particularly from Greek and Roman mythology. Her work often reflected a deep respect for classical sources and a desire to make ancient stories accessible to Victorian and Edwardian readers, especially young audiences.

There was in a small Tuscan village a man named Pomo, who was so lazy that he did not like to work, so he said, "I'll go be a doctor."

So he went into other districts where no one knew him, and said that he could heal people. But instead he only made them die all the more, and at last he died too. One evening soon after his death, his relations were sitting quietly in their house when they heard a great noise, and looking out, saw all the air full of crows. This went on for several evenings, with the house surrounded by these birds, which flew hither and thither cawing loudly, and then vanished.

At last came one evening when there were no crows, but they suddenly heard a great clattering of hoofs in the street. They went to the window and looked out and saw a terrible black horse with a man riding on him. The horse came to the doorsteps, put his nose down to the ground, and stood there for quite a while, while the man looked imploringly at the terrified people, but did not speak.

The next evening the horse came again. This time he stood on the threshold, with his nose against the door, but the man did not speak. In the morning the people went to tell the parroco, the village priest, and beg him to save them from the devil, for they were sure the black horse could be no other.

The parroco lived some way off, but he said, "If the horse comes tonight, call me at once, and I will see if I can help you."

That night as soon as the hoofs were heard someone ran off to the parroco, and the rest huddled into the kitchen so that they might not see the dreadful sight.

But the horse came upstairs, and stood there close by the fire with his nose on the ground and the man on the horse hid his face.

As soon as they heard him coming up the people were so frightened that they jumped out of the window, all but one very old woman who feared the fall more than the horse.

Just then the priest came and asked the man, in the name of God, what he wanted. The man answered, "I want mass said for me, that I may have rest in the lowest part of hell."

"Well," said the priest, "I will say it tomorrow."

"You must say it at midnight, with your back to the altar," answered the man, "and if you make a single mistake you will have to go to hell along with me."

"I'll do it for you," said the priest, for he was a brave man, and with that the horse and man went away.

But when they got among the chestnut trees there was a great noise, and flames of fire burst forth, and so the horse and rider vanished. Well, the next day the parroco tried to get someone to serve the mass, but he had great difficulty, as everyone was afraid of making a mistake and getting carried off to hell. At last he persuaded a priest to help him, and towards midnight the two went to the church.

The horse and rider stood in the entrance of the west door, and the two priests read mass, with their backs to the altar. They got through without mistake and the devil and the condemned soul disappeared and were never seen again, but the priest who had served the mass was taken up stiff and dumb with terror, and it was many weeks before he could speak again. The parroco was less affected, but there was a strange glitter in his eyes for some days, and it was long before he could trust himself to talk of that night.

Concerning A Horse

A Sri Lankan Tale

This tale is my version of an original tale by Henry Parker in his book, Village Folk-Tales of Ceylon, Volume 2, published by Luzac And Co., London, in 1914.

Village Folk-Tales of Ceylon, Volume 2 is the second instalment of a three-volume collection compiled and translated by Henry Parker, first published in the early 20th century. This volume presents a rich and varied selection of Sinhalese folk tales gathered from rural communities across Sri Lanka (then Ceylon), preserving the oral storytelling traditions of the island.

Once, in a quiet village nestled among dry fields and red dust paths, there lived a man who owned a horse. One day, he saddled the animal and set off down the path to visit a nearby town. But he cared little for the horse's comfort. The saddle was worn and the padding thin, and by the time he had ridden half the distance, the skin on the horse's back had rubbed raw and broken open into a painful wound. Seeing the animal could go no farther, the man dismounted, took his cloths and saddle, and left the horse there by the side of the path to suffer.

Later that day, an oil trader came walking by balancing jars of sweet-smelling oil on a yoke across his shoulders. He saw the wounded horse, and saw its back red and raw with sores. Feeling a flicker of pity, he dipped his fingers into one jar and rubbed a little oil on the open wound. "That should ease your pain, old boy," he said, and went on his way.

Sometime after that, another traveler came down the road. He was a kind-hearted man, known in the neighboring villages as someone who never turned away from an injured creature. When he saw the horse, he stopped immediately. "What's this?" he said aloud. "Left like this to rot by the road?"

He opened the small cloth bundle he carried and tore strips from it, making clean, strong rags. Gently, he wrapped the horse's wound, binding the oiled flesh with the soft cloth to help it heal. Then, he added another splash of oil to ease the pain, and gave the horse a few pats on the neck.

"You'll be right again soon," he said. "Take heart." Then he too walked on, leaving the animal bandaged and resting in the shade.

Now, not far from the path stood a man who had been clearing a chena, an overgrown patch of land. That very day, he had set fire to the underbrush so he could prepare the soil for planting. The dry grass caught quickly, and as the fire crackled and spread, the wind turned. A few sparks leapt across the path and landed on the wounded horse's back, right on the rags soaked with oil.

At first, the poor beast kicked and thrashed, unable to stand the pain, but the fire was cruel and fast, and the flames bit into its back. In desperation, the horse stumbled to its feet and ran blindly down the path. With every step, the flames grew, licking up its flanks and into its mane.

Ahead of it stood a lush citronella garden, where rows upon rows of fragrant grass used for oil and medicine grew. The burning horse bolted straight into it, panicked and screaming. The dry leaves caught in an instant. Flames spread like water on stone, and before long the whole citronella garden was ablaze.

The man who owned the garden came running. He watched helplessly as fire consumed his livelihood. When the flames were finally out and only ash remained, he gathered his thoughts and went straight to the King's court.

There, before the King, he bowed low and said, "O wise and noble one, a horse, wounded and wrapped with oil-soaked rags, ran into my garden. It was burning, and it set my citronella plants alight. The garden is destroyed. I seek justice."

The King sat in silence, stroking his beard. Then he gave his ruling. "It is not the fault of the man who wrapped the rags, for he meant only to help. It is not the fault of the horse, for it suffered more than any. It is not even the fault of fire, for fire does only what fire does. But you, who cleared a chena near the road and failed to watch your flames, who did not guard your land with a proper fence, well, the blame, my friend, lies with you."

And so the case was settled. The citronella was gone. The horse, burned beyond saving, lay in a field and died soon after. But the tale lived on, passed from mouth to mouth, as a lesson to all who work with fire, and to all who would lay blame before looking to their own hands.

The Two Horses

A Scottish Tale

This tale is my version of an original note by John Gregorson Campbell in his book, Waifs and Strays of Celtic Tradition, published David Nutt, London, in 1895.

John Gregorson Campbell (1834–1891) was a Scottish folklorist and parish minister known for his meticulous collection and preservation of Highland folklore and mythology. Despite his role as a clergyman, he had a deep respect for traditional beliefs and made it his mission to document the oral tales of the Gaelic-speaking communities of the Hebrides and the Scottish Highlands before they disappeared.

Long ago, in the shadow of the Ben Nevis hills, there lived a kindly old farmer named Donal MacCuaig. He was a quiet man, one of few words but much wisdom, and he knew the language of beasts as well as he knew the pattern of the seasons. On his croft, among heather and bracken, Donal kept two horses, one old and wise, the other young and full of fire.

The elder was called Black Mhairi. She was a sturdy Highland mare with a hide like dappled smoke and eyes that held the depth of lochs. She had ploughed those same fields year upon year, her hooves steady even in the boggiest ground, and her pace so even that folk said you could set your watch by it.

The younger was a colt by the name of Bracken, his coat a glossy chestnut, his legs long and full of impatient energy. He had only lately been broken to the harness, and today was to be his first day yoked for ploughing, shoulder to shoulder with old Mhairi.

As the grey light of morning broke through the mist, Donal yoked the pair and led them to the wide field behind the cottage, the one sloping down toward the river. The earth there was thick and rich, good soil for barley, but heavy going for a beast's first day.

Bracken's ears twitched with excitement, and he tossed his mane as he looked across the field. "Och, Mhairi," he neighed, his breath misting in the morning chill, "do you see it? We'll plough this ridge first, and then that one, and the next after that! We'll cover the whole field before the sun's gone west. Once we get moving, we'll be done in no time!"

Old Mhairi blinked slowly, unfazed by the colt's eagerness. She took a deep breath of the peaty air and looked down the length of the first furrow, still uncut, the soil stubborn as iron in the morning frost.

"We will plough this furrow first," she said, her voice low and calm. "Just this one. And when it's done, we'll set our eyes on the next."

Bracken snorted. "But the field is not so large. Look at it! If we strain hard and pull fast, we could finish before the sun is even high."

Mhairi gave him a sideways look. "Aye, and wear yourself to ruin before the second furrow's done. The field may look small to eyes that've never known sweat, but ask my bones, they'll tell you different."

Still, when Donal gave the word, Bracken surged forward with all the fire in his blood. The plough shuddered as it cut into the earth. For a moment, Bracken pulled ahead, snorting triumphantly, his hooves churning up clods of soil.

But soon the harness grew heavy, the yoke chafed, and the unyielding soil dragged at his limbs like stones in his blood. His breath came short. His muscles began to quiver.

Mhairi, steady and patient, kept her pace. Slowly, the plough evened out. The furrow behind them straightened, and together they carved a dark wound into the stubborn field. One furrow. Then another.

By midday, Bracken was sweating and sore, and glad for the short rest Donal gave them under the shade of a hawthorn tree. He drank from the trough and looked back over the field. The lines behind them were neat, even, and deep.

"You were right," he said quietly to Mhairi. "It is slow going."

"It is the going that matters," she replied. "Not the speed. A field is not won by wishes but by every steady step. There's no pride in starting what you can't finish, but plenty in finishing what you start."

And so, shoulder to shoulder, they ploughed until the sun fell behind the far hills. That night, Bracken slept soundly in the stable, wiser than he'd been at dawn.

And it's said that ever after, when young colts were broken to the yoke on Donal MacCuaig's farm, Bracken would watch from the fence, and if they boasted too soon, he'd stamp once and say, "Plough your first furrow first."

Y Ceffyl Dŵr - The Water Horse

A Welsh Tale

This tale is my version of an original note by Elias Owen Campbell in his book, Welsh Folk-Lore, Elliot Stock, London, in 1896.

Elias Owen (1833–1899) was a Welsh clergyman, antiquarian, and pioneering folklorist. A passionate recorder of oral tradition, Owen collected a wide array of Welsh superstitions, ghost stories, seasonal customs, and folk beliefs, particularly those rooted in rural North Wales. He was driven by a desire to preserve the rapidly vanishing folk traditions of his homeland during a time of industrial and cultural change.

Long ago, in the deep green folds of the Cader Idris hills, where the land rises like an old god's shoulder above mist-wrapped valleys, there was a lake known to the people as Llyn Barfog, the Bearded Lake. It lay as still as glass most days, dark and deep, reflecting little but the grey clouds and the gnarled peaks that stood guard over its waters. Few dared go near it alone.

The folk of the village of Bryn Celyn, which nestled in the valley below, had long whispered of strange lights that flared over Llyn Barfog at night, pale blue fires that danced across the surface as if lit by unseen hands. Sometimes, before a man or woman drowned at sea or fell from the cliffs into the foaming rivers below, these lights would glow with an eerie brilliance, and the sound of hooves would echo across the hills, though no beast was seen. Those folk knew all about Y Ceffyl Dŵr, the Water-Horse.

Now, Y Ceffyl Dŵr was no ordinary creature. It took the shape of a magnificent white stallion, with a mane like flowing silver and eyes as dark as the abyss. It would appear to travellers near lonely water, cropping the grass and feigning gentle docility. To a tired herdsman or curious child, it looked like a gift from heaven. But those who dared to mount it were never seen again.

For once astride the back of the water-horse, the rider would find themselves stuck fast. No struggle, nor any cry for help, could free them. The creature would toss its head with a wild, silent laugh, and then, beneath the waves, he would gallop with unearthly speed. Some said he plunged into lake or river, pulling his victim down, down into his drowned kingdom beneath the earth.

One tale still told with a shiver on cold nights is of Elis ap Rhodri, a shepherd's son who lived in Bryn Celyn. Elis was a bold youth, known for laughing at ghost stories and sneering at the superstitions of his elders. He'd climb cliffs that the crows avoided and swim in pools no other lad would dare enter.

One evening, as a storm gathered over the moor, Elis found himself wandering near Llyn Barfog. The air was heavy with thunder, and the wind curled around him like cold fingers stealing his warmth. There, grazing at the water's edge, stood the most beautiful horse he had ever seen, white as cloud-light, unbridled, and calm.

Elis whistled. The creature turned, its eyes catching the dim glow of the stormy sky. Without fear, the boy approached and swung himself up onto its back. No sooner had his feet touched its sides than he felt the truth of the old tales. His legs were fixed. His hands would not let go of the mane. The horse reared high, and lightning cracked the sky in a blaze.

With a scream swallowed by wind and thunder, the water-horse leapt forward, not into the lake, but up the mountainside, galloping over heather and scree, through mists that curled like ghostly hands. Elis cried out, but the storm drowned his voice.

At the summit of Cader Idris, where the mountain kisses the sky, the horse paused, its breath curling like steam. Then it vanished, some say into the air, some say it plunged straight down through the stones themselves. No one ever found Elis again. But for a month thereafter, the lights on Llyn Barfog burned bright each night, and hooves rang like bells across the hills, though no horse trod them.

The people of Bryn Celyn learned to leave offerings at the water's edge, handfuls of oats, a carved wooden bridle, sometimes a single silver coin. They whispered blessings when crossing the lake paths, and never, never spoke the creature's name aloud while near water. For those who knew always said, "The water-horse is a spirit of judgment and mischief both, and he does not like to be mocked."

To this day, they say that if you see a lone white horse near a still lake or dark river in the high hills of Gwynedd, walk the other way. And if you hear hooves but see nothing, turn your coat inside out, throw salt over your shoulder, and do not stop walking until you reach the hearth of your own home. For Y Ceffyl Dŵr rides still, when the mists are thick and the air is heavy with storm.

The First White Flame

A Unicorn Tale

This is my own tale, because a book of stories about horses would simply be incomplete without a Unicorn or two...

In the days before sorrow had a name, when the world was still wet with the breath of creation, the sky had no stars. The world was not empty then, but it was quiet. Trees hummed but did not yet sing. The rivers flowed but knew no destination. And though animals roamed, none yet had dreams.

In the very heart of the world, hidden beneath a mountain with no name, there dwelled a spirit known only as Danu. She was not a god, not quite, nor was she an elf or faerie. Danu was a wish made by the earth itself. Her hair was woven from mist, her eyes were twin moons, and her voice could wake seeds from stone.

Danu tended to the Cradle of Light, a sacred grove wrapped in vines of silver and guarded by lions made of fierce silence. In the centre of this grove grew a single tree, the First Flame Tree, whose blossoms burned with light instead of fire. Each petal that fell from this tree became a star, rising to the sky to guide wanderers in the dark. But the world was still young, and many corners of it were far too dark.

One evening, as Danu sang to the Flame Tree, a strange wind circled the grove. It carried no scent, nor any warmth. It was the wind of forgotten places, the sigh of caves where light had never been born. It whispered to her, "The darkness grows."

Danu paused her song. "What darkness?" she asked the wind.

"The kind that eats dreams," it replied. "It comes from the Hollow North. It devours colour and leaves only ash. Even the stars flee from it."

Danu turned her eyes northward and saw, far beyond the Cradle of Light, a shadow yawning across the world like spilled ink. She knew what must be done.

From the Flame Tree, Danu plucked one final blossom, one that had not yet become a star. It pulsed with silver fire, humming with magical potential. She held it close and whispered into it a song and a story:

"Of bravery without anger,

Of beauty without pride,

Of gentleness without weakness."

Then she wrapped the blossom in a tear of moonlight, placed it on a bed of cloud, and planted it in the soil just outside the grove.

From that enchanted seedling was born a creature the world had never seen. At dawn, the clouds parted, and a creature stepped into the morning. It stood on legs as slender as harp strings and as strong as mountain roots. Its coat shimmered like frost in moonlight. From its brow rose a single horn, spiralled with truth. Its eyes were deep and clear, like the first reflection ever cast in still water.

It was the first Unicorn.

It bowed to Danu, and where its hooves touched the earth, flowers bloomed that had never existed before, bluebells shaped like bells of glass, roses that hummed lullabies, and moss that glowed beneath moonlight.

Danu named him Solamir, the White Flame.

Solamir was not alone for long. From the echoes of Danu's song and the dreams of her ever present companions, the twilight deer, more unicorns were born. Some were silver, some of pearl and lavender, and even golden ones with stars in their manes.

And when the Hollow North crept further, devouring valleys and silencing birdsong, the unicorns marched. But they did not fight with fangs or fire. Wherever they walked, they left behind light, warmth, and memory. The very grass that trod upon remembered joy beneath their steps. They healed the land with silence and stood unmoved before the shadows.

And when the darkness tried to swallow them, it found that it could not touch truth, because a unicorn's horn, born from a blossom of pure flame and planted by a wish, was the one thing darkness could never bend: the beauty of what is true.

Danu watched as the world filled with brightness. Flowers sang. Rivers found their courses. And children, born under starlight, began to dream. Her work was done.

She lay beneath the Flame Tree and sang her final song, a lullaby only unicorns can hear. From her resting place bloomed a grove of white blossoms that still glow at night in certain untouched woods. From those blossoms emerged the Tuatha Dé Danann, the People of the Goddess Danu, themselves spirits destined to protect unicorns as long as there is light in the world.

It is said that unicorns still walk in the places that humans have forgotten to look into, the deep forests, the misty cliffs, and meadows bathed in morning fog. Their hooves leave no mark, their breath smells like lightning and lilacs, and their horn can heal not only wounds, but broken promises.

They come not to be seen, but to remind the world of what it once was, and what it might be again. And if you ever hear the wind whisper your name while you dream, it may be the voice of Solamir, or one of his kin, calling you toward a grove where the first flame still glows.

"For wherever truth walks in silence,

a unicorn walks beside it."

The Unicorn

As an interesting side note, according to Bullfinch's Mythology...

Pliny, the Roman naturalist, out of whose account of the unicorn most of the modern unicorns have been described and figured, records it as "a very ferocious beast, similar in the rest of its body to a horse, with the head of a deer, the feet of an elephant, the tail of a boar, a deep, bellowing voice, and a single black horn, two cubits in length, standing out in the middle of its forehead." He adds that "it cannot be taken alive" and some such excuse may have been necessary in those days for not producing the living animal upon the arena of the amphitheatre.

The unicorn seems to have been a sad puzzle to the hunters, who hardly knew how to come at so valuable a piece of game. Some described the horn as movable at the will of the animal, a kind of small sword, in short, with which no hunter who was not exceedingly cunning in fence could have a chance. Others maintained that all the animal's strength lay in its horn, and that when hard pressed in pursuit, it would throw itself from the pinnacle of the highest rocks horn foremost, so as to pitch upon it, and then quietly march off not a whit the worse for its fall.

But it seems they found out how to circumvent the poor unicorn at last. They discovered that it was a great lover of purity and innocence, so they took the field with a young virgin, who was placed in the unsuspecting admirer's way. When the unicorn spied her, he approached with all reverence, couched beside her, and laying his head in her lap, fell asleep. The treacherous virgin then gave a signal, and the hunters made in and captured the simple beast.

About The Editor

Clive Gilson was born in 1962 into a household steeped in sport and rhythm. His father was a senior amateur and lower-league professional footballer, while his mother, equally formidable, was an award-winning ballroom dancer. Their spirited household didn't just hum with ambition, it danced to it.

After earning a degree in History from Leeds University, Clive took an unexpected turn into the then-nascent world of information technology in the late 1980s. Yet, the call of story and stage never left him. Alongside a thriving tech career, he freelanced as a journalist and book reviewer, earning one small by-line in the national press, and also spent over a decade performing in village halls and professional theatres across the south of England.

A true inheritor of his family's sporting zeal, Clive later pivoted into live sports broadcasting. In the 1990s, he became a trusted rugby 'stato' for the BBC, ITV, EuroSport, and TVNZ, bringing insight and analysis to major tournaments including the Heineken Cup, Six Nations, World Sevens, and Rugby World Cups.

As a writer, Clive has made his mark across genres. His debut novel, *Songs of Bliss*, was published in 2017, followed by *A Solitude of Stars* in 2019. Since then, he has released three acclaimed short story collections, *The Mechanic's Curse*, *The Insomniac Booth*, and, in 2025, *Melodies in Black Ink*.

He is also an award-winning poet and the author of a biography detailing the life of a former professional footballer, namely his father. Since 2018, Clive has served as Managing Editor of the Firesides Tales Project, a global storytelling initiative that has published over 30 collections of folktales, fairy tales, myths, and legends from around the world.

Today, Clive continues to write fiction rich in folklore, memory, and quiet transformation, combining his deep love of narrative with a lifelong fascination with the human spirit.

For more about his work, visit clivegilson.com, where stories are always waiting to be found.

ORIGINAL FICTION BY CLIVE GILSON

- *Songs of Bliss*
- *Out of the Walled Garden*
- *The Mechanic's Curse*
- *The Insomniac Booth*
- *A Solitude of Stars (Cry Havoc, part 1)*
- *A Symphony Of Sorrows (Cry Havoc, part 2)*
- *Melodies In Black Ink*
- *Acts Of Faith*

AS EDITOR – *FIRESIDE TALES* – *Western Europe*

- *Tales From the Land of Dragons* – Welsh Folk & Fairy Tales
- *Tales From the Land of The Brave* – Scottish Folk & Fairy Tales
- *Tales From the Land of Saints And Scholars* – Irish Folk & Fairy Tales
- *Tales From the Land of Hope And Glory* – English Folk & Fairy Tales
- *Tales from Gallia* – French Folk & Fairy Tales

AS EDITOR – *FIRESIDE TALES* – *Northern Europe*

- *Tales From Lands of Snow and Ice* – Scandinavian Folk & Fairy Tales
- *Tales From the Viking Isles* – Icelandic Folk & Fairy Tales
- *Tales From the Forest Lands* – Finnish Folk & Fairy Tales
- *Tales From the Old Norse* – Scandinavian Folk & Fairy Tales
- *Tales from Germania* – German Folk & Fairy Tales

AS EDITOR – *FIRESIDE TALES* – *Southern Europe*

- *Tales From the Land of Rabbits* – Spanish & Portuguese Folk & Fairy Tales
- *Tales Told by Bulls and Wolves* – Italian Folk & Fairy Tales
- *Tales of Fire and Bronze* – Greek Folk & Fairy Tales

AS EDITOR – *FIRESIDE TALES* – *Eastern Europe*

- *Tales From The Samodivi* – Balkan Folk & Fairy Tales
- *Tales From the Land of the Strigoi* – Romanian Folk & Fairy Tales

- *Tales Told by the Wind Mother*– Hungarian Folk & Fairy Tales

AS EDITOR – *FIRESIDE TALES* – *North America*

- *Okaraxta* - Tales from The Great Plains
- *Tibik-Kìzis* – Tales from The Great Lakes & Canada
- *Jóhonaa'éí* –Tales from America's Southwest
- *Qugaaĝix̂* - First Nation Tales from Alaska & The Arctic
- *Karahkwa* - First Nation Tales from America's Eastern States
- *Pot-Likker* - Folklore, Fairy Tales, and Settler Stories from America

AS EDITOR – *FIRESIDE TALES* – *Africa*

- *Arokin Tales* – Folklore & Fairy Tales from West Africa
- *Hadithi Tales* – Folklore & Fairy Tales from East Africa
- *Inkathaso Tales* – Folklore & Fairy Tales from Southern Africa
- *Tarubadur Tales* – Folklore & Fairy Tales from North Africa
- *Elephant And Frog* – Folklore from Central Africa

AS EDITOR – *FIRESIDE TALES* – *Middle East*

- *Tales From The Meddahs* – Turkish Folk & Fairy Tales
- *Tales From The Hakawati* – Arabic Folk & Fairy Tales
- *Tales Told By Balebos & Gusan* – Jewish & Armenian Folk & Fairy Tales

AS EDITOR – *FIRESIDE TALES* – *Asia & The Far East*

- *Tales Told By The Kathaakaar* – Folk & Fairy Tales from India
- *Tales Of The Gùshì Yuan* – Chinese Folk & Fairy Tales

AS EDITOR – *FIRESIDE TALES* – *Animal Tales*

- *Dog Tails* – Folk & Fairy Tales featuring our canine chums
- *Cat Tails* – Folk & Fairy Tales featuring our feline friends
  Horse Tails – Folk & Fairy Tales featuring our equine pals
- *Pig Tails* – Folk & Fairy Tales featuring our porcine friends

Horse Tails – Equine Fairy Tales, Myths And Legends

AS EDITOR – *FIRESIDE TALES – South & Central America*

- *Tales From The Caribbean* – Folk & Fairy Tales from Caribbean islands
- *Tales From Central America* – Central American Folk & Fairy Tales
- *Tales Told From South America* – South American Folk & Fairy Tales

Reviews

I have edited Clive Gilson's books for over a decade now – he's prolific and can turn his hand to many genres. poetry, short fiction, contemporary novels, folklore, and science fiction – and the common theme is that none of them ever fails to take my breath away. There's something in each story that is either memorably poignant, hauntingly unnerving, or sidesplittingly funny - *Lorna Howarth, The Write Factor*

*Ragged A**** Ruffian* reviewed on Amazon in the United Kingdom on 27 January 2021 - A truly heartwarming, interesting, story with a wonderful narrative. Unquestionably a splendid read

A Solitude of Stars: With deft turns of phrase and an imagination that would make Philip K. Dick jealous, Gilson foresees a dystopian future, the seeds of which are definitely being sown right now. The story is a chilling glimpse of what may come to pass, warmed by a thread of love that raises the narrative beyond despair. I found the stories disturbing and breath-taking in equal measure. The Apparat and Dirigiste tribes are ranging across our solar system seeking peace by waging war, raising the question; is humanity actually capable of peace? A riveting read. - *Rob Swan, The Write Factor*

Songs of Bliss gripped me from the start - I had to read right to the end. Loved the humour. Impressed by the surprising empathy that I felt for rather - on the face of it - unlikeable characters. Look forward to seeing it in print. - *Maighdean-Mhara, commenting on Authonomy*

I just wanted to thank you once more for your help acquiring this beautiful collection. It's found a new home at the top of my library. I've already stumbled onto some wonderful stories in a couple of the collections, and I can't wait to get more. Have a wonderful holiday and a great new year... - *Richer Daniel Laporte, California, December 2021*

Melodies In Black Ink: A collection of darkly captivating short tales, each inspired by the melodies that move us, the lyrics that linger, and the stories hidden between the notes.

Gilson (editor of the international Fireside Stories series) offers a dark, poignant collection of genre-crossing stories, all inspired by songs, that explore the fragile intersections of love, loss, resilience, and the shadows we carry. Ranging from children with superpowers to accounts of blossoming love, abusive relationships, unexpected pregnancies, and the isolating rhythm of a machine-driven society, Gilson's stories capture raw textures of the human experience in a key suggested by their musical inspirations, which include lushly brooding tracks from Kate Bush, This Mortal Coil, Angel Olsen, The Cure, and Youssou N'Dour (the sublime "7 Seconds," a duet with Neneh Cherry.) Gilson has a gift for moment-to-moment storytelling that grips and then lingers, like Gorilla Glue stuck to one's fingertips, resisting even the harshest solvents of reason.

Life goes wrong in unpredictable yet resonant ways throughout these 26 compact tales, and Gilson's vivid portrayals of scenery and emotion make it easy to lose oneself in these narratives, drowning in a wave of feeling that refuses to let go. From the Scottish Highlands to space travel to the blood-soaked earth of Danish-Viking battlefields—told from the perspective of Ulfhednar and his sacred wolf, Ulric—these stories span wide imaginative terrain. Despite some big ideas and SF elements, characterization is compelling. "The Jakey and the Nae Chancer" introduces Elliot and Fiona, who have perfected the art of detachment, the latter of whom "was almost certain that her heart was too delicate to risk breaking again." One of the most heart-wrenching stories, "Be Well," is inspired by a devastating loss. It's a piece that does more than tug at the heart, it reaches in and seizes hold with unrelenting intensity.

Adding a unique dimension, each story concludes with a toast to the song and artist that inspired it, an invitation to experience these briskly potent stories on another sensory level, with a soundtrack tying words to melody, emotion to rhythm. Melodies in Black Ink is not light reading—but it is deeply moving, with haunting emotional rewards.

Searing, surprising stories of urgent feeling, inspired by beloved songs.

Horse Tails – Equine Fairy Tales, Myths And Legends

The US Review of Books
Professional Reviews for the People

Melodies in Black Ink: This work is not just another set of tales linked together by a myriad of characters who sometimes appear in more than one narrative. In fact, this is much more than just another short story collection. It is also a reflective, musical journey. Accompanying each story is an explanation of the song that inspired the writing. Most impressive is the wide expanse of musical genres, artists, and songs included in this book. From Wardruna to Metric to Blue Oyster Cult to Dot Allison, the book's audience will experience a musical journey unlike any other. The incorporation of the notes discussing each inspirational song provides an informative background. It also provides historical context, along with the author's personal anecdotes, about each song.

What makes this book even more realistic is its honest, vulnerable, and sometimes gritty portrayal of the characters and their existences. One story in which all of these themes and characteristics culminate is "Going Underground." It is a story in which even the main character's name, Daniel Grimes, reflects the character's harsh, gritty environment and existence, as well as the difficult decisions Daniel must make. Daniel embodies rebellion against the status quo after having lived a life in which he originally "played by the rules. All it got him were ration credits and a little coin, enough to rent a bedsit and eat slop." "Going Underground" is a daring story with a dystopian tone. Deepening that dystopian tone is the fact that the author cleverly disguises the story's time period, and the tale can be read as either occurring in the past, the present, or the very near future.

Music lovers will appreciate this book because of the role music plays in each and every story. The stories, too, are a testament to not only the power of music but also of the necessity of interdisciplinary studies and the humanities. The stories are a novel type of ekphrastic writing in that, rather than responding to visual art, the stories are responses to music. The fluid, poetic writing in each story mirrors the magic and lyricism inherent in the songs the author utilizes. These stories are powerful, emotional, and moving. Most of all, they are beautifully and unquestionably human.

RECOMMENDED by the US Review

Book review by Nicole Yurcaba